Jonnath stepped into the blood-soaked arena behind his opponent, Yissor. One of the armed guards handed Yissor a tank that had a flexible hose attached to it. Yissor laughed at Jonnath.

"Why sonny, ain't you never seen a flamethrower before?"

Jonnath's scalp tingled, and he swallowed hard. "What . . . what do they give me to fight with?"

"I thought I straightened you out on that. You don't get nothing but the clothes you were born in." Yissor flicked a switch and a tiny flame appeared in the nozzle.

Jonnath was thinking; thinking fast. Survival—a brief lifetime of his father's efforts to teach him survival—this would be the real test.

And to survive . . . he would have to kill an old man.

Would he be able to?

Would he have the chance?

SPECIAL DELIVERY
KRIS NEVILLE

STAR GLADIATOR
By DAVE VAN ARNAM

BELMONT BOOKS   •   NEW YORK CITY

SPECIAL DELIVERY—STAR GLADIATOR

A BELMONT BOOK—October 1967

Published by
Belmont Productions, Inc.
1116 First Avenue
New York, New York 10021

PRINTED IN THE UNITED STATES OF AMERICA

Contents

Dedication

STAR GLADIATOR

to Lee Hoffman

SPECIAL DELIVERY

By Kris Neville

1

A CANNONADE of shell fire met the silver listening post as it zipped across the moonlit desert. It twisted erratically, trying to dodge. Then a radar controlled gun chuckled to itself, and the listening post faltered in flight, slipped air, plunged sandward.

In the Advanceship, far above and to the west, one of the Knougs pressed a button and the listening post exploded in a white flare.

Afterwards, no fragments could be found. The newspapers said the usual thing. The government issued the usual profession of disbelief—and finally even the gunner became convinced of the usual explanation: he had tried to pot Venus.

While on the Advanceship the Knougs continued to prepare for D-Day.

2

THREE DAYS later, on D-Day minus thirty, the Advanceship began to move eastward, seeding down advancemen toward strategic centers in North America.

Towns with big post offices.

7

And then on over the Atlantic toward other continents.

Parr was the first advanceman to land. The coat tails of his conservative suit fluttered gently as he fell; air, streaming by, fretted his hair. Except for the anti-grav pack strapped to his back, he could easily have been mistaken in a more probable setting for an Earthman.

Minutes later his feet touched the ground with scarcely a jolt. He peeled out of the anti-grav pack, pushed the button on its disintegrator time fuse and dropped the pack. He lit a cigar and blew smoke toward the cold bright stars.

He walked from the weedy lot to the nearest bus stop. No one else was waiting. Darkness had concealed his descent. He sat down, stared stolidly at the darkened filling station on the opposite corner.

When he was halfway through the cigar the Los Angeles Red Bus came by and he stood up, boarded it, fumbled in his pocket for change.

"Thirty cents, buddy," the driver said.

Still holding the cigar, Parr counted out two dimes and two nickles. He tried to hand the driver the coins, which were excellent imitations, as was his suit, his cigar, and all the rest of the Earth articles.

"Put it in the box, buddy."

Parr obeyed.

"Hey," the driver said as Parr turned. "Your check." The driver held out a strip of red paper.

Parr took it.

"No smokin' on the bus, buddy."

Parr dropped the cigar and mashed it out. He shuffled down the aisle, sank into a seat and half closed his eyes.

Furtively, then, he began to study the occupants—his first near-at-hand contact with the natives. At the same time he tried to form a mental liaison with some of the other advancemen.

For a moment he thought he had one to the east, but there was a hazy swirl of interdiction that erased all contact.

Abandoning further attempts he tried to search out the frequencies of the minds about him. Once he managed to touch a series of thoughts innocently concerned with household details and with an overtone of mild and name-

8

less anxiety. Aside from that he received nothing except the din of electronic impressions at the extreme lower end of his range.

He half-turned to stare out of the window. The passing landscape was peaceful in starshine and the buildings stood proudly defenseless. In imagination he saw the illuminated, "You'll take a shine to this fine wine" sign hanging askew over a backdrop of smoking rubble. And it was delicious to know that this would be fit and proper.

Although the preliminary intelligence report (based on nearly four years of preparatory scouting) contained no instance of Oholo activity on the planet, he listened, high up, on their frequencies, (particularly here, vulnerably near their own system it would be no fun fighting them). He let his shoulders slump with relief, let the smile of satisfaction come. As reported, the frequencies were clear: Earth was, indeed, their blind flank.

He closed his eyes, relaxed completely, took quite a joy in the knowledge that shortly Earth would be the lethal dagger pointed at the heart of the Oholo system.

At the Beverly Hills transfer-for-Hollywood—the—film —capital—of—the—world Station, two drunks boarded the bus and settled in the rear, singing mournfully.

Parr grew increasingly irritated by the delay. When the bus finally started, making the sharp turn from the lot and throwing his body to the right against the steel ledge of the window, he cursed under his breath.

The dismal singing went on. It picked up telepathic overtones, and Parr gritted his teeth trying to block out the bubbling confusion that scattered from the drunken brain. He opened and closed his fists. Anger flared at him: the anger of impotence. For a moment, he dared to imagine the planet contaminated, the population quietly dead, the Knougs working from sheath hangers. Only for a second; but the brief thought was satisfying, even as he forced himself to agree with the strategy of the War Committee: which was to leave the planet as nearly unpoisoned as possible by even a minor land war.

Finally the song bubbled to silence. Half an hour later the bus turned on Olive Street and the gloomy Los Angeles buildings hovered at the sidewalks. It pulled in at the Olive Street entrance of the Hill Street Terminal and Parr got out.

He walked out of the lot and started downhill toward the Biltmore Hotel.

When Parr awoke he knew that something had been added to Los Angeles during the night. He shivered involuntarily and tightened his thoughts down to the place where no fuzzy, side harmonics were possible.

He was afraid—the startled afraidness of finding something deadly underfoot. Gradually he made his body relax; gradually he quieted his twin hearts; gradually he corralled his breathing. Then he let out a wisp of thought as tenuous as mist.

And he sensed the Oholo's mind again. Very near to his own. He closed his mind quickly, waited breathlessly to see if the Oholo had detected him. His ears hummed with danger for he was within mental assault range.

There was no answering probe and after a moment he got up cautiously.

Feeling the rug beneath his bare feet made him wince with a blind associational terror which he could not immediately analyze. Then, looking down, he thought of the tickle of Tarro fur. He half expected to see the dark stains on the rug too. Always, on Tarro fur—remembering—there were those stains. They had been a difficult people to rule. As *agent provocateur,* (that had been several years ago on Quelta) he had reason to expect blood.

He crossed to the trousers neatly folded over a chair. In the left front pocket was the comset. He fumbled it out and standing naked in the gloomy dawn, whispered: "Parr. There is an Oholo in my hotel."

After a pause the comset issued the tinny question: "Is he aware of you?" The voice filtering through the small diaphragm was without personality.

"I don't think so."

There was silence. Then: "Is he open?"

"I think . . . he is, yes."

"Find out for sure!"

The comset was cold in Parr's hand. He stood shivering. He rubbed his left hand over his naked flank.

He tried to kill his thoughts against the command from the Advanceship, tried to let the drilled in obedience take over. He opened the receptive portion of his mind as far

10

as it would go, knowing that within seconds seepage would be as loud as thunder because he was not adept at double concentration. But even before one second had gone he snapped his mind closed again.

The Oholo was open.

"Parr," he whispered hoarsely into the comset. "He's open."

". . . He can't know we're here, then. What did you learn?"

Parr mopped his forehead with the back of his hairy arm. "I just kept receptive a second."

"Keep checking, then."

Parr let the comset fall to the chair. He walked to the window and looked out at the haze bound city. Early sunlight fought blue smog. Across the street the Pershing Square pigeons waddled self-consciously about on the grass beside the new fountain, picking at invisible tidbits and cooing.

Parr rubbed his throat trying to massage away the inner tenseness. He was alone against the Oholo. An aloneness that he had not been prepared for. And he worried at the fear that was inside him.

He dressed with awkward fingers and left the room, his eyes darting suspiciously along the corridor as he drew the door closed behind him.

He walked quickly down the carpeted stairs and through the front doors of the hotel. Several times he glanced over his shoulder as he hurried toward Sixth Street.

After four blocks he was sure that he had not been followed. He entered a restaurant. He ordered, reading from the menu.

He did not enjoy the meal.

After eating he took a cab to the office of R. O. "Bob" Lucas, Realtor. The Advanceship had determined that Lucas was the agent for an empty warehouse on Flower Street.

Parr exposed a bulky wallet for Lucas' benefit and began to rustle bills with blunt, stubby fingers. Within minutes he had signed a six month lease.

After making an appointment for three o'clock Tuesday at the warehouse, Parr left Lucas' office and caught a cab to a typewriter shop. He purchased a Smith-Corona port-

11

able; a ream of corrasable paper, a disk eraser, and five hundred business envelopes. At the bookstore next door, he bought a United States Atlas.

After that he took a cab to the post office, had the driver wait while he rented six postal boxes under the name A. Parr and bought twenty sheets of air mail stamps.

In the cab once more, he concentrated on the city map that had been impressed electronically on his brain. "Drive out Sixth Street," he ordered, being very careful of his enunciation.

A half dozen blocks out Sixth, Parr located a hotel on the right side of the street. It was a reasonably safe distance from the Biltmore. He ordered the driver to stop.

The building sat atop a hill, the street before it twining briskly toward the center of town. Parr studied the building for a moment, memorizing details of architecture for reference.

Then settled with his purchases in a front room on the 3rd floor, Parr opened the Atlas to the Western United States and marked out the territory assigned to him with the heavy ink lines of his pen.

Having done that, he listed all the names of the included towns.

Then he sat down at the portable, inserted a sheet of paper and wrote:

"To the Chamber of Commerce, Azusa, California. Gentlemen: Please send me the current city directory." He looked at the postal numbers. "My mailing address is . . ." He typed in the first number on the list. ". . . Los Angeles, California. Inclosed is five dollars to defray the costs. Thanking you in advance, A. Parr."

He studied the letter. It was a competent job of typing. He flexed his fingers, found them slightly stiff from the unaccustomed work.

He ran his eyes down the list of towns, inserted another sheet of paper.

"To the Chamber of Commerce . . ."

He stopped typing.

He sat before the typewriter imagining the number of directories, imagining the staggering total of individual names.

He thought of the Advanceship and its baffling array of

12

machines that would automatically scan the directories and print a mailing label for each of the names. He thought of the vast number of parcels waiting to be labeled, as many as fuel requirements permitted the Ship to carry. And of the even vaster number that the synthesizer was adding out of the native resources. The smooth efficiency of the Advanceship, the split second timing of the whole operation . . . And all of it auxilliary timing to the main effort. Even with superior weapons, even with complete surprise, the Knougs were taking no chances. The job of the Advanceship, the job of Parr, was to demoralize the whole planet just before the invasion. To insure an already certain victory.

He turned back to the typewriter, wrote a few more words.

There was still the awareness of the enemy Oholo in the back of his mind.

He split the list of cities into six equal groups for box numbering.

Several hours later another tenant complained about the noise of the typewriter. Parr gave the clerk fifty dollars and continued to type.

3

PARR spent the morning of Tuesday, D-Day minus 28, in his hotel room, reliving what seemed now to be the extremely narrow escape of the previous morning. He imagined what he *might* have done: assaulted the Oholo mentally, or struck him down with the focus pistol when he tried to leave the hotel. And having imagined the situations he proceeded to explain to himself why, instead, he had fled.

At eleven o'clock, by prior arrangement, he reported to the Ship and from it received the reassuring information that the now alerted advancemen had been able to find no other Oholo.

At noon he went out to eat and then for an hour walked the streets, studying the people and their city. Most particularly he listened for accent, intonation. He

13

was afraid to drop his mind shield to try for telepathic contact with them.

A few minutes before three o'clock in the afternoon his cab drew up to the warehouse. The air was hot and sour smelling and Parr was restless. The realtor was waiting for him on the sidewalk. Parr nodded curtly. The man bent clumsily and rattled keys at the lock.

"Here it is," Lucas said.

Parr walked into the warehouse.

It was an old building. Perhaps shabbier, dustier than he had expected. The air was stale and faintly chilly with decay. Remnants of packing crates, wrapping paper, labels and twine had been heaped in a greasy pile in a far corner.

Parr sniffed suspiciously as his eyes darted around the room.

Across from him, above the rubbish, an electric box indicated that the building had at one time been industrialized at least to the extent of a few heavy power tools.

Parr walked to the stairway.

"I'll want someone to clean this mess up," he said curtly.

"Yes, sir," the realtor said.

"Tomorrow," Parr said.

"All right," the realtor said, consciously omitting the "Sir" as if to reassert his own individuality.

Parr glanced at him. "I'll send you sufficient money to cover the fee." Without waiting for an answer, he started up the stairway.

The upper two floors were in much the same condition as the first. From the third there was a narrow flight of steps slanting to the roof. Parr eyed it with disapproval.

"Narrow," he said.

"There's seldom any reason to go up there . . . sir."

Parr went up. At the top of the flight, he forced back the door and clambered into the shed which opened onto the roof. Parr dusted his knees. He stepped outside, and the gravelly finish grated under his shoes. The air smelled of warmed over tar.

He tugged restlessly at his chin. It was a good, substantial roof. As the listening post had reported. Good

14

enough for pickup and delivery. He permitted himself a glimmer of satisfaction.

He heard movement behind him. Instinctively he whirled around, his hand dipping toward his right coat pocket, the memory of the Oholo—the vision of a composite Oholo face surprisingly like an Earth face—flashed across his mind. The realtor's head bobbed into view, and Parr relaxed his tense muscles.

"How is it up to here?"

Parr rumbled an annoyed and indistinct answer and turned once more to the roof. When the realtor stood at his side, Parr said, "I want that shed thing ripped off and a chute installed, next to the stairs. Have it done tomorrow."

"I'm . . ." the realtor began. But he looked at Parr's face and licked his lips nervously. "Yes, sir," he said after a moment. "Anything I can do. Glad to oblige."

"That's what I thought," Parr said, and Lucas shifted uneasily.

Parr turned to the stairs. Going down he could see dust motes flicker in the fading light at the dirty west windows.

Outside he watched the realtor lock the doors.

"Keep the keys," Parr said. "Send them to me at the Saint Paul Thursday morning. At eight o'clock."

The realtor said, ". . . Yes, sir."

At six o'clock Parr was in his hotel, undressed, making preliminary arrangements by telephone to hire a fleet of trucks. He had already placed an advertisement for shipping clerks and common laborers in *The Times*: interviews Thursday from ten to four at the Flower Street warehouse.

After finishing with the truckers, he phoned four furniture companies before he found one open. He ordered it to deliver a desk and two dozen folding chairs to the Flower Street warehouse Thursday morning at nine-thirty.

All the while the Oholo was in the back of his mind, now sharp with sudden memory, now dull with continued awareness.

He checked the schedule the Ship had given him.

He took the comset, flicked it on. "Parr. I'm scheduling. I'll need a packet of money along with the dummy bundle. Can you deliver them both to the warehouse tomorrow night?"

"We can."

15

"Good," Parr said, swallowing, and there was perspiration on his upper lip.

"Have you contacted the Oholo again?"

He felt his blood spurt. "Not yet," he said.

He waited.

Then: "Think you can handle him mentally?"

Parr glanced at the mirror, saw how taut his reflection was.

"I'm not very sure," he said.

"Well, physically, then?"

Parr let out his breath slowly. "I don't know."

"Try. Either way. Get rid of him. An Oholo could cause the invasion trouble."

Parr plucked nervously at his leg. "If I'm not able to?"

The comset was silent for a moment. Then the impersonal voice said, "If you are killed in the attempt, we will replace you." It paused for a reply. Receiving none it continued: "Get what information you can, even at the risk of exposure. It's too late now for them to mount a defense, and they probably have no way to alert the natives. We want to know what he's doing there, and if there are any more on the planet."

"All right," Parr said, and he realized, gratefully, that, to the Ship, his voice would sound emotionless.

He dropped the comset. His hand was shaking.

Not so damned good. How to kill the Oholo?

He tried to steady his nerves by remembering other planets, other times. He had faced danger before, and he was still alive. Except that before the danger had never been an Oholo. He had been Occupation, not Combat. He remembered the few captured Oholos he had seen. They died slowly when they wanted to be stubborn.

Finally he crossed to the bed and stretched out naked, relaxing slowly, knowing that the time had come to get what information he could. Muscle by muscle he began to go limp.

Slowly, very slowly, he dissolved his mind shield. When it was completely gone he began to inch out, to flutter out, concentrating with all his power a stream of receptive thought on the Oholo frequencies high up and uncomfortably shrill.

He located the mind, far away, and he began to skirt in

16

toward it, his own mind trembling in anticipation of the blow if he were detected.

He inched closer trying to make himself completely nontransmitive. He could feel seepage around the beam, and he shunted it to a lower frequency, holding it there, suppressed. The effort blunted his full concentration and when he finally began to get Oholo thoughts they were blurred. He picked up a scrap here, a scrap there, his body tense.

When he relaxed at last, forming his shield solidly, he was weak. He held the shield desperately, chinking it against a possible attack. None came. The Oholo was still completely unsuspecting, completely lulled by the security of its environment.

Feeling a sense of elation and a new confidence, Parr went to the comset. "Parr. Oholo report."

"Go ahead."

Parr concentrated on the wording, filling in the blank spots with his imagination. Suddenly he was conscious of an inadequacy, something elusive that he should be able to add. He wrinkled his face, annoyed. But the uncertainty refused to resolve itself into words. "His name is Lauri. He's here on a mission having to do with the natives. I got no details, but it doesn't directly concern us, I'm sure of that. There appear to be several more on the planet. They seem to avoid cities, which accounts for the fact that advancemen haven't reported them." For a moment, he almost placed his thoughts on the elusiveness, but again it escaped him. He paused, puzzled.

"We'll have the advancemen warned. This may be damned inconvenient, Parr. If there are many of them."

"I couldn't get the exact number without exploring his mind. If I'd done that, I might not have been able to report afterwards."

"Go on."

"He's leaving the city in a few days. You still want . . . me to try to kill him?"

"Yes."

The Oholo, Parr could not help remembering, had as strong a mind as he had ever encountered.

Wednesday morning Parr walked to the Biltmore, not hurrying, not anxious to face a free and dangerous Oholo.

At the side of the hotel he risked contact. A shutter movement of thought told him the quarry was still inside the building.

He crossed Olive at Fifth with the light and angled right into Pershing Square. He located a seat from which he could observe the entrance of the Biltmore. For one moment he considered mental assault; but remembering how strong the mind was he faced he discarded that course.

He waited. He walked around the Square. The morning seemed endless.

Finally he risked another shutter of thought.

The Oholo was still there.

Noon.

He ate in a drugstore across the street.

As the afternoon wore on, the weariness of waiting left his body and the success of the shutter contact inflamed him with confidence. He could cross the street, enter the hotel, seek out the room. But he delayed—without admitting to himself that he was still afraid.

The gloom in the air was pre-sunset, city gloom, nostalgic. He consciously dilated his pupils to accomodate the fading light, unaware now of the scurry of people on the sidewalks and the roar of the city cloaking for night amusement. Neon lights came on like cheap fire, out of the darkness, infinitely lonely.

He shifted uncomfortably. He stood up. He could wait no longer.

Then a man and woman emerged from the hotel. And he tensed. A wisp of thought, unsuspicious, floated to him on mental laughter.

The Oholo, Lauri.

He shielded his mind even tighter, scarcely thinking.

He began to amble in the direction the couple were taking, keeping to the opposite side of the street.

At Sixth they turned toward him, waited through the yellow for the green light. They crossed.

He paused studying a Community Chest sign, his heart pounding uncertainly. He felt a curious little probe of thought that was delicate and apologetic, as if reluctant to intrude upon anyone's privacy. It passed him by undetecting.

The man bent toward the girl, a pert blonde, and

18

laughed in answer to something she had said. Parr watched them go by and then at a short distance swung in behind them. He touched the focus weapon in his right hand pocket, a crystal-like disk with one side tapering to a central point. It was a short range weapon, palm aimed, fired with an equally exerted pressure on the lateral sides.

Even with his mind closed Parr could catch ripples of Oholo thought: amusement, sympathy, appreciation. For a moment he was afraid that he had been mistaken somehow, for again there was the elusiveness, an unreality he hould not account for in terms of the situation.

Parr narrowed the gap between himself and his prey.

And they turned a corner. Parr crossed the street, drew still closer, in time to hear the girl say, laughing, ". . . slumming once before I go back."

The crowd thickened and Parr found himself side-stepping passersby. He was almost near enough, and his hand was moist on the focus gun.

The couple turned into a cellar nightclub. Parr swore to himself. Taking a nervous breath, he descended the steps. He nodded to the bouncer-doorman who was leaning idly against the wall.

He stepped into the nightclub. He saw the man help the girl to a table.

Parr brought out his hand. His eyes were suddenly hot and beady with excitement.

On the far side of the room he saw the black lettered sign, "MEN." He would, in crossing to it, pass directly by the Oholo's table.

As he began to move forward a woman stumbled unsteadily against him, knocking him off balance.

"Whynacha watch where ye're goin,' ya . . . ," she began shrilly, but, with his left hand, he brushed her out of his way. She took a half step backwards, undecided.

He turned to glare at her and under his gaze she looked away and tugged nervously at her dress.

Parr walked swiftly toward the rest room, his every energy concentrated on his mind shield.

As he passed the table, the girl shuffled uneasily on the chair.

Without breaking stride, Parr fired the focus gun into the man's back.

19

He was clear of the tables when he heard, from behind, the initial surprised, "Oh!"

He had one hand on the door marked "MEN" when he felt the confusion in his mind. Automatically, he pushed open the door. A puzzling realization that something was wrong . . .

He turned left, from the narrow corridor into the rest room proper.

And he went down to his hands and knees on the filthy tile, writhing in agony.

4

THE HURT, mostly, was in his brain, and he choked back a scream. He could not think. And then the outer edge of the shield began to crumble.

He concentrated. Every muscle, bone, nerve. Veins stood out on his neck. He fought.

He was dented by fire inside his head. Hot, lancing tongues of flame. He tried to shrink away. He whimpered, groveled. His hands fumbled uselessly.

She was nearly inside of him now. It was almost over. Her thoughts were like fingers rending and tearing at quivering unprotected flesh.

He struggled hopelessly, retreating under a mental assault of unendurable ferocity. His outer memory was ripped away, a section of his childhood vanished forever.

And then there was desperation in the assault wave. He could feel her trying to shake off an attempt to breach her concentration. He stiffened, relaxed, arched his body, struggled with her.

Her attack suddenly crumbled into a distracted muddle. Her concentration had been shattered.

His mind was trembling jelly, creamed with throbbing pain. But he could resist now, and slowly he forced her out.

"I'll be back!" she lashed at him. And the hate in the thought was alive. "I'll kill you for this!" Then her thoughts began slowly to fade away and her mind shield came down.

Parr shook with every muscle.

"Buddy. Buddy," someone was saying, shaking his shoulder. "You sick, huh?"

He struggled to his knee twisting his head back and forth, trying to regroup his memories. The sear places were vacant, empty, part of himself cut cleanly away. Immediate memories not yet stored and filed seemed to be floating free, unassociated—too widely spread to have been cut out, not too wildly spread to have been mixed and shuffled. He was panting as he struggled with them, capturing them, tying them down, ordering them.

Then he began to vomit.

"You drink too much? Hey, buddy, you drink too much? I guess you drink too much, maybe?"

Understanding—half understanding—came with the words. He scrabbled up the wall until he was erect. His back pressed against the vertical tile for support. He turned and staggered from the stinking rest room, his hands forcing clumsily against the walls.

In the short hallway he could hear voices.

"And when he slumped over . . ."

"She just sat there like she was *thinking* . . ."

"You see the cop shake her?"

"I thought she was gonna hit him with the ash tray."

"Well, they sure hauled her outta here!"

Parr staggered back into the nightclub. Eyes turned to stare at him. His head spun in nausea. He began to move leadenly toward the exit.

There was a police officer in his path.

The officer reached out to stop him, and he tried to shake the hand away from his shoulder. He tried to think, to reactivate his trained responses, knowing that he would have trouble with this man.

He muttered wordlessly.

The officer looked grim.

"Not drunk," Parr gasped. "Sick." The officer was incredulous.

Parr shook his head, and an explanation appeared from the basic psychology of the natives: a coded scrap, death fear.

"It . . . it . . . was horrible . . . seeing him like that."

The officer hesitated.

"One minute he was alive, the next minute . . ."

21

"Yeah. Yeah. You better get a cab, buddy."

"Fresh air. I'll be all right, with fresh air."

Suddenly sympathetic, the officer helped him up the stairs.

Once outside the wave of sickness began to recede. Parr waited unsteadily while the officer signaled for a cab.

As he got in the cab he whispered, "Drive."

The driver looked suspiciously at his fare, but the policeman said, "He's sick, that's all. He's just sick."

The driver grunted, meshed gears.

"Where to, Mister?"

"Just drive," Parr said tonelessly, rolling down the window until he felt air hitting his face. He lay back against the seat cushions.

Balloonlike, memories floated, rose, fell. He struggled with them. Drifting away, his hotel's name. Before he lost it, he bent forward, muttered it at the driver.

The Oholo—a female, he knew now—suddenly whispered in his mind from a distance: "You killed the wrong one, didn't you?" He struggled with his mind shield in terror, finally got it set against her. He shivered.

At the hotel, he stumbled from the cab, started in.

"Hey, Mister, what about me?"

"Eh?"

"Money, Mister. Come on, pay up!"

He fumbled at his wallet, found a bill, handed it over.

In his room at last, he peeled off his suit, his underclothes.

He lay prone on the coverlette.

After hours, or what seemed hours, his mind was stable enough for hate.

He lay in the darkness hating her. Even above the instinctive fear he hated her.

He tossed in fever thinking of after the invasion when she would be captured. The last of the sickness ebbed away. His thoughts adjusted, found more and more stability.

Slowly he drifted toward sleep which would heal up the confusions. As he hovered in the dark of near sleep, he felt a wash of mental assault from too far away to be effective. Her thoughts tapped at his shield and he dissolved it partly to let a little defiance flash out.

"I'll get you!" she answered coldly.

And after that, he slept, healing.

He awoke, automatically assessing the damage. It was less than he had expected. Sleep had resolved it into tiny confused compartments.

And he knew how hard it would be to keep up his shield for four weeks. There was fatigue on it already.

Then, too, there was the pressure.

A gentle insistent pressure. As if to say, "I'm here." He remembered how strong Lauri's mind was and he knew that she would be able to hold the pressure longer than he could hold the shield. Once, in training he had shielded for nearly thirteen days—but now, under the sapping of his energy by physical activity, by the multiple administrative problems, by the pressure itself . . .

He shook his head savagely.

He looked at his suit across the edge of the bed. He shuddered with the memory of his sickness and reached for the phone to order new clothing.

And the pressure. He was going to have to learn to get used to it.

Later, he reported to the Ship, his voice fumbling and hesitant.

The answer crackled back. "She's alerted the others, you idiot! We picked up her message. There's four more of them down there."

Parr tried to think of an excuse, knowing how pointless it would be even to offer one.

"You should have used your head," the Ship continued. "What made you think the Oholo was necessarily male?"

"I . . . I don't know. I just did."

"You know what happened on Zelta when an advanceman was careless? You want that to happen here?"

"I . . ."

On Zelta? He knew it should be familiar to him. He cursed inwardly, reaching for other memories, to see how many he had lost . . . A sentence, unbidden, flashed across his mind: "Never sell an Oholo short." It was what someone had told him once. "They think differently than you do." How, he pondered confusedly, could they expect him to think like an Oholo?

"I can't think like an Oholo," he said tonelessly.

"You could . . . Never mind."

"I could? Listen, how can they be thinking, to leave a flank like this unprotected? Why didn't they take this planet into protective custody long ago? How can you *think* like that? They aren't logical. How could I know they'd let a woman . . ."

"Parr!" the Ship ordered sharply.

Parr gulped. "Sorry."

"Insurbordination on your record."

Parr clicked off the comset.

Damn! he thought angrily.

There was still the annoying pressure on his mind. "Damn you!" he thought without lowering his shield. "Damn you!" he thought again, dissolving enough of the shield to let the thought escape.

She did not answer.

There was a knock at the door.

A man with his suit.

It was almost ten o'clock when Parr arrived at the warehouse. The windows were alive with sunshine, and through them he could see the freshly cleaned interior.

The men with the furniture were waiting, the driver angry at the delay, his assistant indifferent. Already there was a line of job applicants who shifted uneasily, eyes turned curiously upon Parr as he crossed and unlocked the warehouse doors.

Parr, one hand resting on the knob, said to the delivery man, "Bring the stuff inside."

The driver growled and picked up a clipboard from the seat. "I gotta bill here, doc. You wanna pay before I haul the stuff out?" He held out the clipboard, jerking it savagely for Parr's attention.

Parr glanced at the sum. He reached for his wallet. One by one he removed the bills and handed them over to the driver. When he had met the amount there were only two bills remaining.

"Now take them inside."

"Okay, doc."

Parr went immediately to the roof. The shed had been knocked down as he had ordered, and the chute had been installed.

24

The two packages were lying at the top of the chute. The bundle of money and the sample, dummy parcel— both night deposited from the Ship. He picked them up.

Walking down the stairs, he peeled away the wrapper from one bundle, exposing green sheaves of currency. Back on the ground floor he put the stacks of bills on the newly arrived desk, and the dummy parcel in the drawer. He took one of the chairs, carried it to the desk and sat down.

He looked toward the door.

"You, there! At the head of the line! Come here." He was careful of his accent, realizing the necessity of impressing the waiting workers. He was pleased to find the accent near perfect.

The woman, frail and elderly came forward hesitantly "My name is Anne, sir."

"All right," he said, reaching for a bill from the top sheaf. "I forgot to bring a pen and paper. Take this and go get some. You may keep the change, and there'll be another bill when you get back."

Her eyes widened. "Yes, sir." She held out a wrinkled hand.

He did not need to glance toward the door again to know that an initial and important impression had been established.

After she had gone, Parr leaned back in the chair and said to the other applicants, "You may come in now."

They shuffled inside.

Parr watched them settle into chairs. As he did so, he was aware of *her,* Lauri, holding the pressure steady on his mind, and memories of last night came back. Concentrating away from them he tried to analyze his feelings toward the natives. He found a mixture of contempt and indifference.

"I'm going to say this only once," he announced crisply. "I will expect you to inform any latecomers. When I have finished I will interview each of you."

He balanced his hands before him on the rim of the desk, holding them steady. He looked around at the waiting faces. He let his mind relax and the speech—it had been graven on his brain in the Ship—came bubbling to the surface. He searched forward along it, and he found it to be complete, untouched by his contact with the Oholo. He wrinkled his forehead and began, seeking to give the impression that each word was being carefully considered.

"I intend to hire some of you to help me sort and load packages of promotional literature. Those hired will be paid five dollars an hour."

They shuffled unbelievingly. "Yeah, but when, Mister?"

Parr's mind dipped for information. "Whenever you wish to. At the beginning of every day. Will that be satisfactory?"

The listeners twisted uncomfortably, embarrassed by their doubt. "Now you're talkin'," the original critic said.

Parr cleared his throat heavily for effect. "The work day may be as long as fourteen hours, depending on the circumstances."

No questions, now.

"The literature will come already packaged and labeled. It will be delivered to the roof by helicopter, and your job will be to sort it and transfer it to trucks." He looked them over. "I will need you for approximately three weeks."

The pressure was still on his mind, not demanding, merely present. He writhed at it inwardly. Outwardly he was calm, his voice undisturbed.

"Hey, Mister," another of them said. "I'd like to get somethin' straight right now. You ain't havin' us to handle no explosives er somethin' dangerous like that, are you?"

It was an objection Parr had been prepared for. Scarcely thinking, he bent to the drawer and picked up the dummy parcel. He put it on the desk top.

"There is no danger. You will need no special instructions save to handle as you would normal mail. I have a sample package here." He bent over and stripped off a section of wrapping paper to permit them to see a stack of printed material.

He rippled the dummy sheets with his thumb. "The nature of the advertising is secret for the moment, but," he lied, "this is what it looks like." He returned the bundle to the desk. "It's just paper." That was true, and he smiled faintly as he imagined the amount of disorganization mere paper would be able to accomplish. For an instant, the uncertain emotion returned as he thought of the invasion fleet, rushing communicationless through hyperspace for its rendezvous with Earth.

"There is, of course, a reason for the high wages," he said, the words coming automatically. "We want to hit the market before—ah—" and the phrase and the hesitation were memorized, calculated for effect, "a competitor."

He pursed his lips speculatively. "Naturally we want to avoid publicity. Anyone violating this requirement will be dismissed immediately."

He seemed to study the faces individually, looking for spies from the rival company.

"I will probably not require you for more than a few hours the first several days. In that event, you will receive pay for a full eight hour day."

He stopped talking, and the applicants' faces were excited.

"As soon as the woman returns with the paper, I will begin the interviews. Those of you whom I hire will receive a fifty dollar bonus before you leave the building."

When she returned, Parr interviewed. His questions were perfunctory. By noon, he had enough workers, and he had one of them hang out a penciled sign reading: "Jobs Filled." After that, he closed the doors and assembled them before him.

"If you'll form a line, I'll give you your bonuses. Give me your names to check against my list. You will sign a sheet of paper here in receipt. I've hired enough people to take care of any of you who do not choose to come back tomorrow, so there will be no further vacancies and no chance to collect a second bonus . . . Report for work at nine o'clock tomorrow morning. At that time, I'll have someone here to fill out the necessary government employment forms for each of you."

Sitting at his desk, he began to count out the bills into neat little stacks. After each applicant had signed, he pushed a stack toward him.

After that he spent the afternoon making further arrangements with truckers and locating a woman to handle the employment records of his workers. He even had time to purchase some extra clothing and buy a few personal articles.

27

As night fell, while he lay comfortably naked on his hotel bed, he felt the pressure on his mind begin to fluctuate subtly.

5

THE OHOLO, Lauri. Strong-minded, yes. But untrained.

And realizing this, Parr smiled, for it testified to the certainty of his superiority, a superiority he should have recognized from the beginning. He was dealing with an amateur, an Oholo who had never received even the most elementary instruction in individual tactics.

What she was doing now was glaringly obvious to a professional: cruising the town in an attempt to locate him. But in contacting his shield by focusing the pressure, directionally, she failed to realize that the space variations would not only tell her of his location but also inform him of her movements.

Cautiously Parr began the defensive procedure. Step by step he engaged the pressure with his mind, rather than letting it rest on his shield. Then he began to counteract the distance pulsations—strengthening, weakening, presenting a continual pressure against her questing thoughts, compensating for her movements.

But in a very short time she realized what had happened. She altered the pressure sharply. A split second later he joined it again. The advantage was still his. She altered once more. He followed suit. Check.

He could almost feel her angry confusion. Then after a moment she let the pressure fall into a rhythmic pattern. A lullaby of montony that was the result of concentration rather than of the distance variations. He knew what to expect and after fifteen minutes it happened. She broke the rhythm suddenly and tried to plunge inward, to center on him before he could counter. He had not been lulled, however, and she accomplished nothing. He met the assault easily.

The rhythmic pattern returned. Every few minutes she broke the pattern and tried to plunge in again. But his mental screen absorbed the shock.

She was persistent.

Finally Parr grew weary of it—then vaguely annoyed —then exasperated.

When he was thoroughly uncomfortable she tried another swift change of tactics. She began to increase the pressure, slowly, inexorably—stronger and stronger against his defense. He blocked her, held, retreated, held again, keeping the shield in readiness. Shortly, perspiration stood on his forehead. Abandoning the defensive he fought back against her.

But she blocked him; they locked in a deadly mental tension of spiraling energy that weakened Parr with each passing second.

She held the tension longer than he would have thought possible. And when it eased, it vanished, leaving his mind uncontacted. Instead of relaxing, he formed his shielding, expecting a sudden assault.

None came. Instead, the gentle insistent pressure returned, undiminished by her efforts. She was stationary now; the pressure was steady.

His body had been tense for a long time. It ached, and he was physically exhausted. His hand shook a little as he brushed at his leg, waiting for the space variations to begin again.

They did not.

But the initial confidence—generated by the realization of her inexperience—was no longer so bright.

The very pressure itself now was an emotional drain and he wanted to lower the mind shield and relax completely. But even at a distance a mental assault would sting like a slap, like a cut, like disinfectant in a raw wound.

Under the strain, sleep was lost. Instead there was uneasiness.

He tried to ignore it. He forced himself to remember his home village. It had been a long time since he had thought of it, and at first it was difficult. But after a while, memories began to open up with nostalgia: the clumsy citizens with their mute opposition to the Empire, a *jehi* farmer who had once addressed his class on planetism and afterwards been shot, the smell of the air, the look in people's eyes, night . . . the stars . . .

The stars were cold and bright and far away. Imposing symbols of Empire.

His mind turned comfortingly on that, and his planet seemed dwarfed and unimportant. The Empire, with its glittering capital system, the sleek trade arteries . . . the purposeful masses of citizens . . . the strength and power of it, the essential rightness of it. Something you could feel in the air about you and smell and see. It was a thing to be believed in, to be lost in, to surrender yourself to.

It was strong, crushing opposition, rolling magnificently down the stream of time—splintering, shattering, destroying, absorbing, growing hungry and eternal. He was part of it, and its strength protected him. It was stronger than everything. There could be no doubt about Empire.

But a single Oholo was strong, too.

He stirred restlessly on the bed, unable to dissect out the thing that bothered him when he thought of the Empire. His thoughts had run the full cycle, and they were back where they had started.

It seemed for a moment as if his mind were a shiny polished surface, like an egg floating beneath his skull, hanging on invisible threads of sensation that ran to the outside world.

The room was full of moonlight.

With fascination he studied the wall paper, a flower design scrawled repetitiously between slightly diagonal lines of blue. He concentrated on the rough texture of the paper, let his eyes drift down to where the paper met the cream siding, revealing twin rifts of plaster. A thin line of chalklike dust had fallen on the wood of the floor. The edge of the rug, futilely stretching for contact with the wall, curled fuzzily.

A faint breeze fluttered the half drawn blinds, puffed the lace curtains, rippled in to his bed and body.

He was guilty of something.

He wrinkled his face, puzzled. What was he guilty of?

No answer, and the moon went behind a cloud, bringing depression and acute loneliness, sharp and bitter. A depression bleak in its namelessness, and terrifying.

Then suddenly his mind jerked away from the thoughts.

He realized he was not countering the Oholo's movements. The steady pressure was a compensated pressure, varying as her distance. A projection requiring mental ability he could never hope to equal. She had learned fast. She had neatly sidestepped his defense. Terrified, he probed beyond his shield, and for an instant received an impression of her distance. He sat upright, shivering. She had worked much nearer. In desperation, he launched an assault, closing his eyes, forgetting everything else.

Lightly she parried him and slapped back strongly enough to make him wince.

Then for two long hours they fought. He grappled with the pressure, working on the theory that it was a burden no mind could carry indefinitely.

But she did not concede. Instead she continued, giving up trying to come closer, intent on breaking down his will to resist. He checked her with all his energy. He countered, stared at the scattered moonlight on the rug.

Energy drained from him until he wanted to scream, to plead with her. And beyond the bleak reality of concentration he knew that she was using twice as much energy as he was.

Then she began to weaken. The pressure steadied, and he could feel her exhaustion. She was through for the night.

The sheets of the bed were damp. His body trembled. He wanted to whimper pathetically in fancied defeat.

Sleep slowly came, and the long pervasive influence of Empire, the influence visible in concrete form on conquered planets, swept over him.

But somehow he was guilty of something, he knew . . .

He was still tired when he awoke, instantly alert, wary. She apparently still slept, although she held the pressure against his mind.

Dawn ushered in a cloudy day, and street noises—cars, buses, movement—came into the room with the utmost clarity.

He would have to change hotels. That alone had an urgency to it. Wearily he fumbled with his shield. It was still solid. He ran a hand over his forehead, pressing against the temples.

He thought of the sleeping Oholo. He dropped the shield completely, knowing she would realize its absence. He stretched mentally for a long, precious second, and it was with infinite relief.

"Hello," he leered in the direction of Lauri. "Hello," he snarled suddenly, tingling with excitement.

No answer.

"Hello! Hello! Hello!"

He shielded, and hatred of her and of all Oholos—inbred hate, overcame him. It brought an almost pathological bravado with it. The destructive drive for revenge was a surge within him. He dropped the shield and thought to her, slow and gloatingly, of the things in store for her when she was safely disarmed and helpless. And he permitted his hate to leap and caress her, and the details of the torture were etched in passion acid.

After a while, he could feel her shudder at the thoughts, and he simpered. She seemed to lie helpless, stunned under him, spurring him to greater imaginative excesses.

Then she struck out blindly, a shivering blow that caught him unaware between the eyes like a swung club.

He shielded. Instantly he felt the guilt of last night. He was angry at himself, as if he had acted without really wanting to, as a Knoug was supposed to act. And he snarled a curse.

The maddening, uncompromising pressure returned. Implacable. Patient. Unanswerable. Pressure that would drive him insane if he had no eventual hope of release. He shuddered, and the sense of depression—the night sense—was even more dark and terrible in daylight.

He got out of bed, reported to the Advanceship, keeping his voice low and even.

"Parr. Scheduling."

"Check."

The voice from the Ship was a stabbing, accusing voice. A voice that *knew,* that had made, overnight, a secret and awful discovery about him. He wanted to grovel before it and pleaded for forgiveness . . .

Nonsense!

He licked his lips nervously.

"That damned female!" he shrieked.

"Eh?"

"That damned female, don't you see!"

"Parr, what's wrong? Listen, Parr, are you all right down there?"

Suddenly he relaxed. "Nothing. Nothing's wrong."

32

"Are you sure?"

"Yes," he said. "I'm just a little nervous."

He ordered the driver to stop. The building was columned, red brick, decayed. The sidewalk before it was grimy, littered, cracked, chipped. Listlessly, people shuffled down the street, flecks from the vortex of humanity farther uptown drifting in the backwater of the city. Faded overalls, jeans, thin unpressed cheap suits, frayed shirts and crumpled soggy collars. Faces—lean, hollow, blotched; eyes that were harried, red, tired. The women, still trying to retain the snap of movement, were like wind-up toys, almost run down.

Parr grunted at the smells of the area, and straightening up to pay the driver, noticed distastefully the slack faces, defeated eyes and shuffling steps.

Then he knew: here, pressing in from all sides was reassurance. He watched a haggered face, felt pity, shook off the emotion as unworthy but still felt it. He could understand the haggard face. But distaste returned again, for he was superior to the face. He blocked off his mind, refusing to consider the natives any longer . . .

He took a room inside the dingy, wasted building. He hung his extra suit in the closet. The wall was greyish with cracking plaster and water stains, half hidden by the dim light; the rug underfoot was threadbare and stale. On the dresser, a Gideon Bible, nearly new.

The sheets, he discovered upon turning back the bed, were dingy and yellowish. The mattress sagged in the middle and the metal bedstead was chapped and dented.

After he was settled he reported to the Advanceship, told of his new location and the reason for it.

On his way out of the hotel he was conscious of the guilt again, and in the street, he stopped an old man who wore a tobacco stained shirt and gave him several of the bills from his wallet. Bribing helplessness made him feel better.

Back in the hotel that evening, renewed confidence came as he thought how clever he had been to choose such a location; he thought of the Oholo searching across town, her mind automatically rejecting this location. It would take her more than one night to find him.

But her mind did not seek contact with his; instead,

the pressure remained annoyingly general.

She was making no attempt to locate him.

He stared out the window at the pale reflection of neon from the sidewalk. She was not even moving yet.

He waited, suddenly nervous.

When she finally began to move she still kept the pressure general.

He checked her position and after an instant met opposition that scattered his thoughts. But in that space of contact he knew she had moved closer.

In terror he drew his shield in tight.

Suspense mounted in his mind.

He counted his pulse beats, quieting himself. He tried to relax. Then fearfully checked her position again. That involved receiving a sharp slap of assault, for she had been ready with an almost trigger response.

And she was closer. She seemed to be advancing confidently.

In nervous haste he began to dress.

And then she struck with her full hellish power from very near at hand.

Amazement and abject fear flamed in his mind. He fought to strengthen the shield. She forced it back, got a single hot tentacle of thought through into his mind proper, and it lashed about like a living thing before he could force it out.

Gradually he came to realize that she was not near enough for the kill.

He staggered to the door, his mind numbed and spinning as if a giant explosion had gone off by his ear.

And then, somehow, he was in the street, half dressed. Somehow he managed to find a cab. It was all a blur to him that might have taken two minutes, five minutes, or twenty minutes. She had not abandoned the assault. She was moving closer.

Then, before the cab began to move he saw her. Two blocks away. Coming toward him. Her face was impassive, but even at a distance, the eyes . . . or was it his imagination? The focus gun . . . in his pocket . . . The cab drew away. He leaned out the window, twisting back, tried to aim at her. The shot, silent and lethal, sped away. The distance was too great.

Then a new assault, but it was too late. He held it until

34

the cab outdistanced it. She renewed the pressure and he could think again. And he knew, in the back of his mind, that soon now they would meet. And he shuddered, wondering of the outcome.

He was sick. Unbelievably, she had outguessed him. She had guessed he would flee away from the obvious to the other extreme.

His breathing was hoarse and painful, and he thought comfortingly of his home planet; a small planet with a low sky; incredibly blue, a trading station far removed from Earth, satisfying deep in the Empire. As a boy he had often gone to the space port to watch the ships. He remembered how he had stood watching their silvery beauty and their naked violence. He had always been very excited by them. Always. And they were a symbol of Empire.

After the cab driver had spoken to him several times he roused himself to say, "A hotel, any hotel."

It was luck he knew, that he had been beyond effective range. She might have guessed the correct slum hotel and stood below his window.

His mind was foggy and befuddled.

And he had been hurt. Much more than mentally hurt. More than physically hurt. He wanted to hurt something in return. Only now he was too tired.

He relaxed in the seat, listened to the hiss of tires. He would be able to sleep tonight. She could not figure out his next move, predicted on random selection.

In his new hotel room he found that his body stung and itched.

And she began to search for him.

He had to fight her for more than an hour, and after that he slept, subconsciously keeping his shield on a delicate balance.

6

THE NEXT DAY Parr went first to the post office and from there immediately to the warehouse. He brought with him three manila envelopes containing three city directories, the first responses to his requests. He took them to the roof, checked the three cities off his list, placed the directories at the base of the chute. Later the helicopter would come swishing down from the night sky, collect them, and return tomorrow evening with the compressed and labeled parcels, one to a family, stamped with the requisite postage. The parcels, spilling out of the compressor, would expand to a huge jumbled heap for the natives to handle. And Parr knew he was only one of many advancemen. The cargos would nightly spew to all points of the Earth from the Advanceship slowly circling the globe behind the sun.

Complete coverage was what the Knougs were aiming at. Here advancemen were using the government postal system for distribution; there, making arrangements for private delivery; elsewhere, setting up booths. Earth had been scouted very thoroughly by four prior Intelligence expeditions. It was an inconceivably complex network of planning, possible only through extreme specialization in an organization made frictionless by obedience.

That night Lauri's pressure increased—or seemed to—and he shook his head like a hooked fish. He began to walk faster, mumbling under his breath.

The solution, he knew, was distance. A partial solution only, for he was bound by assignment to commuting range, not great enough to permit him to lose her completely.

The jangle and clank of a city train roused him. An interurban bus. It was stopped at the next corner accepting passengers.

He turned and ran the quarter block to board it.

As he rode toward the ocean he could feel the gradual lessening of the pressure; it was a lessening not nearly as pronounced as he would have felt were she trying to center on him as he fled, but sufficient to relax him. He could feel a puzzled pressure shift after a few miles as she checked him briefly, then an over excessive spurt of questing thought which he countered automatically. Even if he only remained shielded it would take her at least a week to localize him except in a very general direction.

He began to feel all of the overcharged tenseness drain out of his muscles. He even began to take an interest

36

again in his surroundings, studying the buildings with appreciation. The incongruity of the architecture was more apparent than before, due to his greater acquaintance with the thought patterns of the natives.

A bizzare sight: a temple in the style of the Spanish, low-roofed, unpretentious, comfortingly utilitatian with no nonsense except for the gleaming gold minaret atop it, its coiled surface outlined with neon tubing.

It drifted away, behind.

Here a huddled shop, antique-filled and sedate, less than a block from a brilliant drive-in in disk form, radially extending like a somnolent spider.

And most paradoxical of all, the false glamor of signs encouraging the spectator to rub shoulders with excitement that was supposed to be inside the door, but wasn't. For people who were incapable of finding it anywhere. Parr felt suddenly sad.

Odd natives, he thought. But even odder thoughts for a Knoug, he knew. Then he felt the savage stirrings inside of him again. It brushed away sadness. The numbered days until the invasion excited him. The emotional surge of danger and trial and obedience were the preludes to the necessary relief.

Parr felt fully relaxed.

He got off the bus in Santa Monica, where the night fog was already fingering in from the ocean.

He crossed the wide street, angled toward the Mira Mar hotel.

In his room he stood looking out across the street over the stretch of park that broke suddenly as a dull cliff, dropping jaggedly to the road beneath. Beyond were buildings unusually small and squalid in sea perspective. The beach, curving north to Malibu; and the sea itself was overshadowed toward the Ocean Park Pier by the brazen glitter of red neon.

But the fog was quieting the scene, and isolating it. After a bit there was no world beyond the window but the grey damp world of fog.

Still the excitement beat at him. He projected his thoughts beyond the immediate future to the bright burning of the Oholo System, the atomic prairie fire skipping from sun to sun at the core, leaving the planet ashes—while isolated, the periphery worlds would one by one capitulate to Knoug power, to Knoug *will,* and become infected with Destiny.

Beyond that?

The doubt came, and he cringed mentally.

He was guilty of something.

His hands whitened on the sill, and staring into the fog he tried to bring all of the weight of Empire to his support.

But there was the memory of revolt by Knougs themselves on a tiny, distant moon.

The depression came back.

. . . It took the Oholo four nights to locate him.

7

THE STRAIN on his face—the heaviness of his eyes— the taut lines of his throat. His body was exhausted.

Like dripping water the pressure pounded at him.

The night before, she had found him at Long Beach.

He cast off the depression to find euphoria; and the two alternated steadily with increasing peaks.

His hands were nervous. Blunt thumbs constantly scrubbed blunt fingertips in despair or anticipation.

. . . The trucking had all been arranged for.

The deliveries from the Ship occurred nightly. He had sent follow up letters to cities who had not responded to his first request. The answers had finally arrived.

The warehouse, floor by floor, was filling. Already some trucks were waiting.

There was the continual bump of handled packages sliding from the chute, being sorted, being stacked. But worries piled up inside of him: fears of an accident, a broken package, a suspicious employee, a fire . . . The Oholo, the guilt, the depression.

Eagerly now he listened to the general information report from the Ship. Most advancemen were on schedule. No irreparable accidents. Certain inaccessible areas had been written off. A few advancemen recalled for necessary Ship duty. One killed, replaced, in Germany. World coverage estimated at better than seventy per cent in industrial and near industrial areas, a coverage probably exceeding the effective minimum—short only of the impossible goal.

He had been talking to a trucker in front of him without really hearing his own words, his fingers and thumbs rubbing in increased tempo.

He hated the man as he hated everyone in the building, everyone on the planet.

The trucker shrugged. "I'll have to deadhead back. That has to go in the bill, too."

"All right," Parr snapped irritably. "Now, listen. This is the most important thing. Each of the lots has to be mailed at the proper time. Your bonus is conditional on that."

"Okay," the trucker said.

"I can't overstress the importance of that," Parr said. He handed the slip of paper across the table. It was a list of mailing information, Ship compiled, that was designed to assure that the packages would all be distributed by the mails as near simultaneously as possible.

"You deliver the Seattle lot, that's number, ah, eighteen on the list, the last."

"I understand."

"When your trucks are loaded, you may leave. I'll pay you for layover time."

"I've got a bill here," the trucker said.

The two huddled over it, and after the trucker had gone Parr leaned back staring at the ceiling, his nerves quivering.

He knew what he was guilty of, at last. Knowledge came suddenly, from nowhere like an electric shock, and it stunned him. Logically he demanded proof; but there was no proof. It came, it was; it was beyond logic. Nothing in his memory . . . and for a moment he thought he had lost the memory under Lauri's first vicious assault ripping into his mind; but, and again without reason, he knew it was not in the memory she had destroyed. She was connected with it, but not like that . . . He was guilty of treason. He could not remember the act, but he was guilty. What? When? Why? He did not know; he was guilty without knowing what the treason was: only the overpowering certainty of his guilt. Wearily he let his head droop. Treason . . .

"Mister Parr?"

"Eh? Eh?"

"There's somethin' heavy in this one. It don't feel like paper. I think it's metal of some sort. Now, look, Mister Parr, I don't want to get tied up with somethin' that's not square. You said all these packages had paper in them. And I'd kinda like to see what else there is in this one, Mister Parr, if you don't mind."

Parr wanted to jump out of the seat and smash at the man's face. But he forced himself to relax.

"You want to open the package, is that it?" he said, gritting his teeth.

"Yes, Mister Parr."

". . . Then go ahead and open it."

Having expected refusal, the worker hesitated.

"Go ahead," Parr insisted. He kept his face expressionless, although, beneath desk top level, his hands bundled into knobby fists, white at the knuckles.

Then at the last possible second, as the worker's fingers were fumbling at the wrapping, Parr leaned forward. "Wait a minute. It won't be necessary to waste the parcel . . . Unless you insist."

The worker looked at Parr uncomfortably.

A question of timing. Events hung in a delicate balance between exposure and safety. Parr reached for the drawer of the desk, his movements almost too indifferently slow.

His hand fumbled inside the drawer. "I think I have some of the metal samples around here," he said. His hand found the stack of gleaming dummy disks, encircled it possessively. He tossed them carelessly on the desk top and one rolled, wobbling, to the edge and fell to the floor.

Puzzled, the worker bent to the one that had fallen, picked it up, turned it over in his hand, studying it curiously.

"I don't see . . .," he said suspiciously.

"That's our product," Parr lied. "We include some in every hundred or so bundles. The literature explains their function."

The worker shook his head slowly.

"As you can see," Parr persisted gently, "they're perfectly harmless." He tensed, waiting.

". . . Yeah, uh . . . I think I get it. Something like them hollow cement bricks they use to cure people of rheumatism with, huh?"

Parr swallowed and relaxed. "That's the general idea. You'll see . . . Well, if you want to, go ahead and open the parcel."

"Naaah," the man said foolishly. ". . . There wouldn't be no sense in doin' that."

Beneath the desk top again, his hands coiled and flexed in anger and hatred. "I want your name," Parr said, a very slight note of harshness in his voice.

The worker let his eyes turn to the backs of his heavy hands, guiltily. "Look, Mister Parr, I didn't mean . . ."

Parr silenced him with an overdrawn gesture. "No, no," he said, his voice normal and conciliatory. "I meant, we might be able to use a man like you in our big plant in the East." He snarled inwardly at himself for the unnecessary note of harshness before: it was too soon for that.

Suddenly stammering with excitement, the worker said, "My name's George . . . George Hickle . . . George Hickle, Mister Parr. I got good letters from back home about my workin', sir."

"Where do you live, George?"

"Out on Bixel . . . Just up from Wilshire, you know, where . . ."

"I meant the number of the house, George."

"Oh." George told him.

Parr wrote it down. "George Hickle, uh-huh."

"I'll be mighty obliged, Mister Parr, if you'll keep me in mind."

"Yes. Well. Good afternoon, Hickle. You ought to be getting back to your work now, hadn't you?"

And when the worker had half crossed the room, Parr drew a heavy, black line through the name. He had memorized it.

The pencil lead broke under the pressure.

And at that moment, the pressure in his mind vanished.

In automatic relief, he relaxed his shielding for the first time in what seemed years, and before he could rectify the error Lauri hit him with everything she had, catching him just as the shield began to reform.

Pain roared in his mind. From the force of the blow he knew that she must be near the warehouse.

It had been one quick trust, leaving his mind throbbing and he sobbed in impotent hate and anger.

The pressure was back.

And slowly and surely she was closing in on him, compensating. She had struck prematurely, realized her mistake, and was narrowing the range, holding the final assault until assured of victory.

He stood up weakly and hurried to the door, brushing through a group of startled workers.

Outside, a cab was cruising, and Parr ran after it. It did not stop. He turned and ran frantically in the opposite direction, rounded the corner, still running, his heels thudding on the hot pavement.

He ran for blocks, the blood pounding in his head, sweat trickling into his eyes. Pedestrians turned to stare, looking back along his line of flight.

When Parr stopped, finally, he was trembling. He stared at his own hands curiously, and then he looked around him.

He swallowed hard. The world swam, steadied. His chest rose and fell desperately . . .

At the airport, he phoned the warehouse.

"Hickle? Get me Hickle . . . Hello, Hickle, this is Parr. Listen, Hickle, are you listening? Hickle, I've got to leave town for two days. You've got to run things. You understand? Listen. I've left money in the drawer of my desk . . . for the payroll . . . You know how to run things, don't you, Hickle? . . Now, listen, Hickle, there's some trucking . . . Wait a minute . . . Look . . . You stay down there. Right there. I'll phone you back, long distance, later. Don't go away, Hickle. Wait right there. I'll tell you what you've got to do."

The last call for his plane came over the loudspeaker.

"Listen, Hickle, I've got to run. I'll phone you later, so wait. Wait right there, Hickle!"

Over Bakersfield, gratefully—infinitely gratefully—he felt the last wisp of pressure vanish.

He was free.

There was no consequence powerful enough to keep him from dropping his mind shield entirely. But he let it come down slowly, barrier by barrier, enjoying the release, prolonging the ultimate freedom beyond.

At last the roar of the motors, muffled, sang in his head like an open song, and there was nothing between his thoughts and the world.

His mind stretched and trembled and pained from the stress, and quivered and fluttered and pulsed and throbbed and vibrated and rejoiced.

He looked out over the wing, through the whirring propellers, at the hazy horizon, at the cloudless sky, bright and blue and infinite.

It was the best day he had ever known. It was freedom, and he had never known it before.

His mind was infinitely open as the sky above the clouds, and he stretched it out and out until he forced the limit, beyond which no mind may go, yet wanting to plunge on.

In the east, there was the dusk of night coming down, a cloak pulled up from the other side of the world by the grapple hooks of dying sunshine.

In San Francisco he phoned Hickle in Los Angeles, a man and a place so far removed that he wanted to shout to make himself heard over the telephone.

Then to a hotel—but now as a place of rest and refuge, not a symbol of flight and fear. His hate returned, beautiful, now, flowerlike, delicate, to be enjoyed. To be tasted, bee-like, at his leisure.

The city outside was a whirl of lights and the lights hypnotized him with their magic. Soon he was in the streets.

There were cabs and scenes: laughter, love, death, passion—everything rolled into a capsule bundle for him. The city spread out below in a fabric of light, the hazy blue of cigar smoke closely pressing sweaty bodies, laughing mouths. A swirl of sensations.

"Somewhere else!" he cried madly to a driver.

China Town, the International Settlement, Fisherman's Wharf . . . The cabbies knew a tourist.

He had been moving for hours, and now he was tired and lost, and he could not find a cab to get back to the Sir Francis Drake.

A girl and a sailor passed. A tall lithe blonde with a pert nose and high cheekbones and brown eyes, heavy lips and free hips . . . a . . . blonde.

The Oholo . . . Lauri . . . was a blonde.

He began to cast up memories of her, sickeningly, making his fists clench.

He wanted a blonde to smile at him, unsuspecting. A blonde with honey colored hair and a long, slim throat with a blue vein in it, so he could watch the heart beat. He wanted to hurt the blonde, and hold her, and caress her softly, and . . . most of all, hurt her.

He wanted to shake his fists at the sky and scream in frustration.

He wanted to find a blonde . . . .

Finally he found one. In a small, red-fronted bar, dimly lit. She was sitting at the end of the bar, facing the door, toying with a tall drink, half empty, from which the ice had melted.

"What'll it be, Mister?"

"Anything! Anything!" he said excitedly as he slipped behind a table, his eyes still on the woman at the bar.

"And the same for me?"

"Sure. Sure."

She brought back two drinks, picked up a bill, turned it over in her hand speculatively. She wore an off the shoulder dress, and high rouge on her Mexican cheeks. She made change from her apron, putting the money beside the second glass, sitting down in front of it, across from him.

Still he had not noticed her.

Two patrons entered. They moved to a table in the far corner near the Venetian blinds of the window and began to talk in low husky voices.

"I'll be back, dearie," the woman across from Parr said, sipping her drink, smearing the glass rim in a veined half moon.

She went to serve the girls.

When she came back Parr had brushed away the drink from in front of him.

"Listen, dearie," she said. "You got troubles?"

He grunted.

She snaked an ample hand half across the table and wiggled her shoulders to show off her breasts. "I bet I know what's wrong with you. Same as a lotta men, dearie. Want a little fun, I bet."

"Bring me that blonde," he said hoarsely.

"Listen, dearie, you don't want her. What you want . . ."

"The blonde!"

Reluctantly she stood up, frightened by his tone. She put a hand over his change, waited.

He did not notice.

She put the money into her apron pocket, heaving her chest.

Then she got the blonde.

"You wanna buy me a drink, honey?" the blonde said.

"Sit down!"

The blonde turned to the Mexican. "Make it a double." She sat down.

"Talk!"

"Whatdaya wan' me to say, honey?"

"Just talk." He had seen the pulse in the vein in her neck. The neck was skinny, and the face was pinched, lined with heavy powder. Her eyes were weary, and her thin hands moved jerkily.

"Just talk."

When she saw his wallet, as he brought it out to pay, she said, "Maybe we oughtta go somewhere to talk." Her voice was flat and nasal, and she tossed her head. She ruffled her coarse dirty-colored hair with an automatic gesture.

Parr wanted to kill her, and his hands itched at the delicious thought.

But not tonight. Not tonight. He was too tired. He . . . tonight he just wanted to think about it. And then he wanted to sleep and rest and think.

She tossed off the drink. "Another one, Bess," she said shrilly, glancing at him.

He took two bills out of his wallet, two twenties, put them on the table, pushed one of them toward her without looking at it.

She drank two more shots quickly, eagerly, hungrily, as if there was need to rush through them and get them safely inside.

She leaned across the table, her eyes heavy. "I'm gonna talk, okay? Man wants to hear woman talk. Get yer kicks

45

like that, okay. You're buyin' . . . Hell, I bet you think I'm a bad girl. I'm not a bed girl—bad girl." Her hands twitched drunkenly below her flat breasts. "There was a sonofabitch in my town . . . I came from up north, Canada." She drank again, hastily. "I could go for you, know what? . . . I'm getting drunk, that's what. Fooled ja, didn't I? Listen. You wouldn't believe this, but I can cook. Cook. Like hell. Wouldn't think that, eh? Hell, I'm good for a lotta things. Like being walked on. Jever wanna wanna—walk on a girl? Listen. I knew a guy, once . . ."

Parr said, "Shut up!" For one instant, there was sickness and revulsion, and desire to comfort her, but it vanished almost before it was recognized.

She closed her mouth.

He pushed the twenty dollar bill into her lap.

"You be here tomorrow. Tomorrow night."

"Okay."

"You be here tomorrow night."

"Sure, sure, honey."

"You be here tomorrow night, and don't forget it." She smiled drunkenly. "I'm here . . . . most nights, honey . . ."

"You be waiting for me."

"I'm always . . . waitin', honey. Ever since I remember, honey, waitin'. Just waitin', honey."

But the next morning, when Parr awoke, Lauri was trying to center on his open mind. She was in San Francisco, looking for him.

The depression came back, and the guilt—the knowledge of treason—that made him want to go to a mirror and stand, watching blood trickle down his face in cherry rivulets like tears.

And fear.

When he shielded, she resumed the pressure.

At noon he was back in Los Angeles. Perspiration was under his skin, waiting icily.

He went directly to the warehouse.

Hickle, in surprise, crossed the room to him. "Mister Parr!" he said.

The right corner of Parr's mouth was twitching nervously. "Get a chair. Bring it to the desk."

46

When Hickle was seated before him, Parr said, "Okay." I've got some papers. I'm going to explain them to you." He got them out. "They're all alike in form. Here." He took off the top sheet and Hickle stood up to see. "This number, here, is for the truck unit." He circled it and scribbled the word "truck." "This number." He circled it. "This number is the lot number. You see, truck number nine has lots seventeen, twenty-seven, fifty-three, thirty-one."

"I get it," Hickle said.

Parr's body was trembling and he threw out a tentative wave of thought probing for the Oholo, afraid that she might come silently, knowing his approximate daytime location. He began to talk rapidly, explaining.

It was D-Day minus seven.

After fifteen minutes, he was satisfied that Hickle understood the instructions.

"There was a plain bundle this morning?"

"Yes, sir. I wondered about that."

"Get it."

Hickle got it.

Parr opened it. "Payroll money, trucker money. Give the truckers their money when they give you their bills. I'm going to trust you, Hickle."

Hickle gulped. "Yes, sir."

Parr began to stuff money into his wallet.

She was in Los Angeles. He knew by the pressure on his mind.

"I've got to hurry. Listen. I want you to keep the workers here as long as necessary, hear? This schedule's got to be kept. And you take a thousand dollars. And listen, Hickle. This is just chicken feed, remember that, when you're working for us."

"Yes, sir!"

He had her located, keeping his mind open to try to center on her.

He could center on her! She was only partially shielded, and she made no protest. She was not moving, and he could . . . except that there was something wrong with the pressure. He was overlooking something. But she was not moving. Not yet.

"I've got to talk fast. All these final deliveries. You'll

47

be busy. If you need help, hire it. And listen, I'll be here from time to time if I can."

"There's something wrong, Mister Parr?"

Parr searched for an excuse. "It's personal . . . my wife, yes, my wife, it's . . ." He wondered why he had used that one. It had sprung automatically to his mind. "Never mind. I'll phone in from around town. I'll try to help you all I can by phone."

She was not moving, but the pressure seemed different . . . *alien!*

He jerked out of his seat, kicking the chair over as he headed for the door.

A different Oholo!

There were two of them in Los Angeles!

He probed out.

Lauri was almost on top of him.

He skidded through the door, into the street, knocking a startled man out of his path.

He stared wildly in both directions. Several blocks away a cab was stalled with a red light.

And almost before him, a private car was headed uptown. With three huge leaps he was on the running board, yanking the door open.

He jerked himself in beside the frightened driver.

He twisted his head, shouting. "Emergency! Hospi . . ."

She had seen him trying to escape. She struck.

In the street, a flock of English sparrows suddenly faltered in flight, and one plunged blindly into the stone face of a building. The others circled hysterically, directionless, and two collided and spilled to the ground.

"Hurry, damn it!" Parr moaned at the driver. "Hurry!"

He slammed forward into the windshield, babbling.

The terrified driver stepped down on the accelerator. The car leaped forward.

Parr, fighting with all his strength, was twisted in agony, and blood trickled from his mouth.

He gasped at the driver: "Cab. Behind. Trying to kill me."

The driver was white-faced and full of movie chases and gangster headlines of shotgun killings, typical of Southern California. He had a good car under him, and he spun the wheel to the right, cutting into an alley; to the

48

left, onto an intersecting alley; to the right, into a cross-town street; then he raced to beat a light.

He lost the cab finally in a maze of heavy traffic at Spring.

Parr was nearly unconscious, and he struggled desperately for air.

Run, run, run, he thought despairingly, because two Oholos are ten times as deadly and efficient as one . . .

8

D-DAY minus four. General mailing day.

Parr, his mind fatigued, his body tense, phoned the warehouse twice, and twice received enthusiastic reassurances behind which he could hear the hum and clatter of parcels being moved, trucks being loaded . . . cursing and laughing and subdued shouting.

How many hours now? His mind was clogged and stuffy and sluggish. An hour's sleep, ten minutes sleep—any time at all. If it could be spent in clear, cold, *real* sleep.

Eat, run. Always, now, he was running, afraid to stop longer than a few minutes. He needed time to *think*.

And the pressure was steady.

Get away. Leave Los Angeles!

"Parr, Parr. This is Parr," he whispered hoarsely from the back seat of the moving cab into the comset.

The rhythm of the engine, the gentle sleepy swaying of the car and the monotony of the buildings lulled him. He caught himself, shook his head savagely.

Dimly he could understand the logic advising him to remain in the city. But it was not an emotional understanding and it lacked the sharpness of reality. For now the two Oholos could follow him easily, determining his distance and direction. If he left Los Angeles, the focus of the invasion, it would be difficult to return after postal delivery. After the invasion it would be nearly impossible. It would give the Oholos added time to run him down. But to remain . . . His body could not stand the physical strain of four more days of continual flight, around,

around, up Main—to the suburbs—to the ocean—back to Main again—down the speedway to Pasadena and through Glendale to Main. Change cabs and do it all over again.

"Yes?" the Advanceship said.

"I'm . . . leaving. I've got to leave. I've got to." And suddenly, in addition to the other consideration, he was afraid to be there when the invasion hit. Was it because he was afraid they knew of his treason? Or . . . was it because . . . he liked the buildings? Strangely, he did not want to see the buildings made rubble . . .

The answer: "You have a job to do."

"It's done!" he cried in anguish. "Everything's scheduling. In a few hours now it'll be all over. I can't do anymore here."

A pause.

"You better stay. You'll be safer there."

"I *can't!*" Parr sobbed. "They'll catch me!"

"Wait."

A honk. The purr of the engine. Clang. Bounce. Red and green lights.

". . . If the mailings are secure, you have the Ship's permission. Do whatever you like."

Expendable.

Parr put the comset in his coat pocket and cowered into the seat.

"Turn right!" he said suddenly to the driver. "Now . . . now . . . Right again!"

He bounced.

He closed his eyes, resting them. "Out Hill," he said wearily without opening his eyes.

He withstood an irritated mental assault. They were tiring. But not as fast as he was.

The silent pursuit: three cars out of the multitudes, doggedly twisting and turning through the Los Angeles streets—separated by blocks, even by miles, but bound by an unseen thread that was unbreakable.

"I gotta eat, buddy."

Parr drew himself erect. "A phone! Take me to a phone!"

The taxi ground to a stop in a service station.

Nervously, Parr began to phone airports. Three quarters of his mind was on his pursuers.

50

On the third try he got promise of an immediate private plane.

"Have it ready!" he ordered. Then, dropping the receiver he ran from the station to the cab.

He jockeyed for nearly thirty minutes for position.

Then he commanded the driver to abandon the intricate interweaving and head directly for the airport in Santa Monica.

Shortly, the two other cars swung in line, down Wilshire.

The job of softening up Earth for the invasion began to pass entirely from the hands of the advancemen. From a ticklish, dangerous proposition at first to a virtual certain mailing day. The world wide mechanism of delivery swung into operation from time zone to time zone, and, in the scheme of conquest the advancemen passed from integral factors to inconsequential objects.

All over America, from east to west, within the space of a single day the post office became aware of the increased, the tremendously increased volume. Previously in certain sections there had been signals in the form of out-bound dribbles. Now there were in-bound floods rising suddenly to the peak intensity of overtime innundations. A million packages, some large, some small, some brown wrapped, white wrapped, light, heavy—no two alike, no way to tell the new influx from the normal handling.

At the very first each office saw the rush as a unique phenomenon—for there was no reason to report it to a higher echelon which might have instituted an investigation. Merely to take care of the rush, that was all. To process the all-at-once congestion of parcels to be door to door delivered. Later to be marveled at.

Lines formed at parcel windows; trucks spewed out their cargos. Lights burned late; clerks cursed and sweated; parcels mounted higher and higher.

Nor did it break all at once in the press. The afternoon editions carried a couple of fillers about how Christmas seemed to be coming early for the citizens of Saco, Maine, and how a tiny Nevada town whose post office was cobwebby from lack of use suddenly found itself doing a land office business.

Most of the morning editions carried a whimsical AP article that the late radio newscasters picked up and re-broadcast. Then after most West Coast stations were off the air for the night events began to snowball in the East.

The breakfast newscasts carried the first stories. The morning papers began to tie in the various incidents and reach astonishing conclusions . . .

The propeller was not even turning over. The plane, wheeled out of the hanger, was waiting, cold, and the pilot lounged by the office, smoking a cigarette.

The sky was black, and here and there before the blatant searchlights sprouting from dance halls and super markets, clumps of lacy California clouds fluttered like dingy sheepwool in a half-speed Mix-Master.

Parr, tossing a handful of bills at the driver, leaped from the cab and ran frantically toward the office.

The wait was terrible. Should the Oholos arrive, he was boxed in spaciously, with no escape. In gnawing at the inner side of his lower lip, he bit through his disguise into real flesh and real blood.

There were forms to sign, responsibility to be waived. And with every minute, *they* drew nearer.

Finally the airplane motor coughed into reluctant life, and Parr could feel the coldness of artificial leather against his back.

The ship shuddered, moved heavily, shifted toward the wind onto the lighted runway. The motor roared louder and louder and the ship trembled. Slowly it began to pick up speed, the wings fighting for lift.

A searchlight from the pier made a slow ring of light toward the invisible stars.

The ground fell away and Parr was on his way to Denver.

Almost immediately, with the pressure still on his mind but fading swiftly, he fell into a fitful sleep and dreamed of treason, while, in the background ominous clouds shifted and gathered to darken the sun of his native planet. Finally, all was a starless black except for half-forgotten faces which paraded before him, telling his treason with hissing tongues in words he could not quite grasp the meaning of.

The air of Denver was clear and bright—crystal clear,

drawing in the mountains, opening up the sky like a bent back box top. The new sun seemed small.

Parr stood on a street corner acutely aware of the thin air and the bright clean sky. An open sky that seemed to be trying to talk to him. He snorted at the absurdity of the thought but he strained half consciously to listen.

He walked on, his feet tapping sharply on the concrete, his mind foggy from the uncomfortable sleep.

A building to the left momentarily reminded him of a slide shown long ago in a classroom on a distant planet, and he wondered if the picture had been taken in this city (knowing, deeply, that it could not have been).

Parr took a newspaper from a stand. Tucking it under his arm he continued to walk until he found a hotel.

He ate breakfast hurriedly in the annex and then rented a room with a radio. He went to it, lay relaxing on the bed, his mind open and free but uneasy again as he thought of treason.

"Parr," he said into the comset. "I'm in Denver."

"Have you escaped?"

"They will follow me," Parr said wearily. "But for the moment, I'm free."

"We'll send our Denver advanceman to you," the Ship said. "The two of you should be able to handle the Oholos."

Parr's mouth was dry. He named the hotel.

"Wait, then."

He lay back but felt no exultation. He tried to force it, but there was nothing.

And then, staring at the headlines, knowledge of success broke all around him and he was trembling and jubilant. He sprang up, paced the room, moving his hands restlessly.

He rushed to the window, looked out into the street. The people below passed in a thin nervous stream. Unusually few; many more were glued at home, waiting for the mail.

A postal delivery truck turned the corner, rolled down the street before the hotel. All action ceased; all eyes turned to watch its path.

Parr wanted to hammer the wall and cry, "Stop! Stop! I've got to ask some questions first! Stop! There's something wrong!"

Parr was shaking. He sat on the bed and began to laugh. But his laughter was hollow.

His victory—a Knoug victory . . . He frowned. Why had he automatically made a differentiation where there should be none? He realized that the mailing success had released him from nervous preoccupation in Knoug work; for the first time he was free of responsibility, and he could think . . . clearly . . . about . . . . He wanted to hammer the terrifying new *doubts* out of his mind. But they gathered like rain clouds. He went to the mirror and fingered his face. "What's wrong? What's wrong?" Knoug victory had a bitter taste.

He suddenly pictured the civilization around him as a vast web held in tension by a vulnerable thread of co-operation, now slowly disintegrating as the thread crumbled. And he took no joy in the thought.

He began to let images float in his mind. Imagined scenes, taking place beyond the walls.

A man went in to pay off a loan, his pockets stuffed with money.

"I'm not taking it."

"Whatsa matter? It's legal tender. You *gotta* take it." Bills on the counter.

"You didn't earn that!"

"It don't matter."

"It isn't any good. Everybody's got it."

"That don't *matter.*"

"It's worthless!"

"Yeah? Listen: 'For all debts, public and private . . .' "

Parr's mind reached out to grasp the unsettling immensity of it. He flipped on the radio, half heard an excited announcer.

Parr thought: All over the world, each to his own: coins, bills, dollars, rupees, pesos, pounds—how many million parcels were there? Each stuffed with enough to make its owner a man of wealth, as wealth was once measured.

Parr thought it was terrifying, somehow.

And the headline of the paper admitted: "No Test To Reveal Good Money From Bad."

(There was a mob. They were storming a liquor store, while the owner cowered inside. He was waiting for the police. But the police were too busy elsewhere, so finally, to salvage what he could before the mob took his stock for nothing he opened the door, crying, "Form a line! Form a line!")

Parr thought of the confusion that would grow.

Prices spiraling.

(In the United States Senate, a member took the floor to filibuster until California had its mail delivery and its fair share of the free money.)

This was the day work stoppages would begin.

FAMINE PREDICTED . . . PRESIDENT IN APPEAL TO . . . GUARD MOBILIZED . . . .

Riots. Celebrations. (A church burned the mortgage gratefully.) Clean shelves. Looming scarcity.

By the time the sun dipped into the Pacific, the whole economic structure of the world would be in shambles.

Governments doubtless would blame each other (half-heartedly), propose new currency, taxes, and the gold standard again.

Industrial gears would come unmeshed as workers took vacations. Electric power, in consequence would begin to fail.

(Looting already occupied the attention of the better part of the underworld, and not a few respectable citizens decided to get it now and store it for use when it would be unavailable because others had done likewise.)

Stagnation tomorrow. But as yet, the fear and hysteria had not really begun. Parr shuddered, sickened. "What have I *done?*"

It would take months to unmuddle the chaos.

Earth was ripe for invasion . . .

Parr aroused from a heavy stupor. The pressure was back. He moaned, and the knock on the door jolted him into startled animal movement.

The knob turned. Parr tensed, although he could tell that the Oholo team was still distant. "Who is it?"

The door opened and a disguised Knoug slipped through. Immediately behind him a simianlike Earthman towered. "Come in," the Knoug said. When they were inside, he shut the door.

"The Ship sent me over," the Knoug said. "You wanted help? My name's Kal. You probably remember me on Ianto?"

Parr swung his legs from the bed and stood up. "You feel the pressure?"

Kal rumbled angrily.

"Two Oholos," Parr said. "I've been dodging them."

"Two, eh? Okay. It's a good thing I brought Bertie along. Two, you say. Well I'll be damned."

Kal turned to the Earthman. "There'll be two, Bertie. So watch yourself . . ."

Bertie grunted noncommittally.

"Okay. Now like I told you, shoot when I give you the mental signal. You'll see the ones."

"Uh-huh," Bertie said, chewing complacently.

"Go on downstairs then."

Bertie hunkered forward and leered at Parr. "Sure. Sure."

"Hurry the hell up," Kal said.

Bertie shuffled to the door, opened it, left the room. Parr swallowed uneasily.

Kal chuckled. "Good one, Bertie. Useful. Damn this pressure. Glad I brought him. They won't be looking for an Earthman, eh? So when they try to come in here after us, he'll drop 'em, eh?"

Parr wet his lips. "They're getting nearer."

"Relax," Kal said. He crossed to the bed and sat down. "The Fleet's out. It just came out. Did you hear?"

Parr felt a shock of surprise. He imagined the hundred powerful ships of the fleet coming, one by one, from the dead isolation of hyperspace. In his mind's eye he could see the faint glimmer of the static shield—the protective aura—from slowly in real space; he could imagine the ships safe within their electric sheaths which caught the hull-wrenching force of transition and dissipated it from the heavy steel plating. He could imagine one ship—perhaps one—popping out, shieldless, battered by the force vortex, and perhaps leaking air or ruptured entirely because the protective aura had collapsed under pressure. Then he saw the ships neatly pulling into formation, grouping for instructions, waiting for the attack signal.

"Day after tomorrow they attack," Kal said.

"They're closer," Parr whispered.

Kal concentrated. "Yeah. I feel them. Come to the window." He stood up and crossed the room in quick catlike strides.

Parr followed him and the two of them stared down. Perspiration stood on Parr's forehead. After a moment they saw Bertie come out from beneath the hotel awning. He seemed small at a distance, and they saw him toss a cigarette butt carelessly to the sidewalk. He moved leisurely away from the entrance and leaned against the side of the hotel, one hand in his overcoat pocket.

Kal sneered, "You think they'll drive right up?"

Parr's face twitched. "I don't know . . . if they know there's two of us . . ." He glanced left along the street. "I guess they will. I guess they'll try to come right in after us."

Kal chuckled. "That's good. That's damned good, eh?"

Parr turned to stare at him. "They're strong."

"They won't be looking for Bertie."

"Listen," Parr whispered hoarsely. "They're stronger than we are."

Kal snarled a curse.

"No," Parr said intently. "They are."

"Shut up!"

"Listen," Parr said. "I know. I've . . ."

Kal turned slowly. "They're not stronger. They *couldn't* be stronger. Even if Bertie misses, we'll get them. If they're so strong, why haven't they already carried the fight to us? If they're so strong, they should be ready to attack us, so why don't they?"

He turned back to the window.

"They're almost here," Parr said.

A cab turned the corner. "Feel them center on us?" Parr said, drawing down his shield as tightly as he could.

Kal, tense-faced, nodded.

Parr stared fascinated as the cab screeched to a halt.

Then Parr felt a wave of sickness and uncertainty; he reached out for Kal's elbow. "Wait!" he cried.

But already, below, Bertie jerked into explosive action.

He shot three times. The male Oholo pitched forward to the gutter.

Bertie's gun exploded once more, but the muzzle was aimed into the air. He crumpled slowly, and the gun clinked to the sidewalk from nerveless fingers.

"He got one," Kal said in satisfaction. "The other one must be quicker 'n hell."

Parr let out a tired sigh.

"That's that," Kal said. ". . . I'll be damned, a female Oholo! She won't dare to try two of us alone."

Parr's eyes were fixed below. In what seemed a dream, he watched her get out of the cab. She glanced up and down the street. She looked up, quickly, toward their window. And then she darted across the sidewalk toward the hotel entrance.

"I'll be damned!" Kal cried. "She's coming up anyway!" His eyes sparkled gleefully. He searched his lips with his tongue. "Let's both hit her now! She's near enough!"

"No!" Parr cried sharply. "No! Let her get closer . . . Let's . . . let's make sure we get her."

They could feel her nearing them, not quickly, not slowly, but with measured steps.

9

SHE WAS just outside the door and Parr felt something like momentary confusion before the hate came. Yet when it did it was tinged and colored as he thought of her walking toward them, alone. He tried to concentrate on her remembered image, tried to call up the previous hate in all its glory. He could not; instead, even the hate he knew drained away. In its place he felt—not fear exactly —not fear for himself but of the inevitability of death. Not his death—hers.

He saw Kal's lips curl, and then he winced. Fingernails dug into his palms.

And the door opened and she stood before them. There was a breathless instant, absolutely still, while time hung fire. Her eyes were aflame. Eyes, he knew, that were capable of softness as well. Eyes steady, intent, unafraid. He was frozen in delicious surprise that tingled his spine, and he felt his scalp crawl. He also felt deep awe at her courage.

She came into the room, closed the door, stood with her back leaning lightly against it. Her eyes blazed into his.

Her red lips moved delicately. "Hello," she said. "I've been looking for you." She had not glanced at Kal.

"Now!" Kal cried wildly.

Parr wanted to scream something meaningless, but before the sound could bubble forth the room seemed to erupt into a colored blaze. She had struck at him with a lethal assault!

He reeled, fighting back for his life, conscious now of Kal fighting at his side.

Her eyes were steady, and her face frowned in concentration. She was icy calm in the struggle and there was cold fury in her whips of thought. But slowly, under their resistance, her eyes began to widen in surprise.

For a breath-held moment, even with the two of them against her, the issue seemed in doubt; Kal half crumpled, stunned by a blast of hot thought that seared away his memory for one instant.

She could not turn fast enough to Parr, nor could she, in feinting his automatic attack, strike again at Kal. Then again, the two of them were together, and slowly, very slowly, they hedged her mind between them and shielded it off.

Kal recovered.

Parr gritted his teeth in a mental agony he could not account for and stripped at her outer shield. Kal came in too and the shield began to break.

The Oholo still stood straight and contemptuous in defeat, her eyes calm and deadly as she still struggled against them.

She struck once more with fading strength and Parr caught the thrust and shunted it away. And then he was in her mind.

He held a stroke that would burn like a sun's core, and almost hurled it. But there was a great calmness before him and he hesitated a fraction of a second in doubt as he stared deep into her glazing eyes. He felt his heart throb in new pain.

Kal struck over him, and the Oholo went limp, suddenly, and sank unconscious to the floor, a pathetic rag doll. A tiny wisp of thought struggled out and faded.

Kal cried in triumph and gathered for the final blow.

Great, helpless rage tore at Parr then, and almost before he realized it he sent a powerful blast into Kal's relaxing shield. Kal rocked to his heels, dazed, and his left hand went to his eyes. He whirled, lax mouthed, surprised.

"What . . .?"

"She's mine!" Parr screamed wildly, "She's mine!"

"The hell—"

In fury Parr slapped the other Knoug a stinging blow across the mouth. "Get out! Get out! Get out or I'll kill you!"

Kal's eyes glazed in surprise.

Parr was panting. "I'll finish her," he gasped. "Now get out!"

Kal's eyes met his for a moment but they could not face the anger in Parr's.

"Get out or I'll kill you!" Parr said levelly, his mind a welter of emotions that he could not sort out and recognize.

Kal rubbed his cheek slowly. "Okay," he said hoarsely. "Okay."

Parr let breath out through his teeth. "Hurry!"

Kal's lips curled. His shoulders hunched and he seemed about to charge. But Parr relaxed, for he saw fear in the Knoug's eyes. Kal straightened. He shrugged his shoulders indifferently, spat on the carpet without looking at Parr and stepped over the unconscious Oholo. He jerked the door open and without looking back slammed it behind him.

Parr was trembling and suddenly emotionally exhausted.

Parr's knees were water. He stared fascinated at the fallen Oholo. He sank to the bed. He let his thoughts touch her unconscious mind as it lay exposed and helpless, and he wondered why he did not strike the death blow. He tried to think of stripping her mind away slowly, layer by layer, until she lay a helpless babbling infant, her body weak and pliant to his revenge. But he thought of her clear eyes and he was sickened and ashamed.

He called up memories of Oholos—the captured few—and now for the first time he knew general respect rather than hate. And thinking of Knougs, he writhed.

Yet he was conditioned to hate and he was conditioned to kill. He must kill, for the conditioning was strong. He tried to fight down the revolt of his thoughts, and, in recognizing the revolt at last, knowledge came. The guilt of treason. Not for any act. His treason was doubt, and doubt was weakness, and weakness was death. He could not be weak for the weak are destroyed. But he seemed, for a heart beat, to see through the fabric of Empire which was not strength at all. No he thought, I've believed too long. It's in my blood. There's nothing else.

He went to the wash basin and drew a glass of water. He carried it to the Oholo, knelt by her head and bathed her temple with his dampened handkerchief until she moaned and threw an arm weakly over her forehead. Her hand met his, squeezed, relaxed, and was limp again.

He carried her to the bed and sat beside her, staring at her clear face, which was an Earthface. (I've been in this body too long, he thought, I'm beginning to think all wrong.) For the face was not without beauty for him.

He shook his head dazedly, trying to understand himself.

(Here is the enemy, he thought. How do I know? I have been told ever since I can remember. But is it true? Does saying it make it true? But what else can I believe? One must believe something!)

She opened her eyes, stared at him uncomprehending. He waited patiently as she gathered her loose thoughts and tied them down. She smiled uncertainly, not yet recognizing him.

Finally he could see understanding in her eyes.

"Your mind is too weak to fight," he said. "If you try to shield I will kill you."

Her lips curled. "What do you want?"

"Don't try to shield," he warned. He studied her face and his chest was tight. He looked away from her face.

"I've got to ask you some questions," he said. "After that, I'm going to kill you."

There was no fear in Lauri's eyes. "Go ahead," she said calmly. "Kill me."

"I . . . I . . . want to ask you something first," he said. "I've got to ask you some questions."

Her lips glistened and he felt sympathy that he could not understand. And seeing her frown, he shielded the thoughts from her.

"You're not . . . quite like I thought you were," she said, very calmly.

"I am!" he snarled. "I am what you thought!" He was

61

ashamed of the sympathy he had let her sense, and then he was ashamed of being ashamed, and his mind was confusion.

"Why did you—did you leave this planet as an unprotected flank, like this?" he said. It was a question, he knew, that had to be answered, before . . . before . . . what?

"They weren't ready to join us," she said.

"What do you mean?"

"They were not developed enough to join us," she said.

"Why didn't you conquer them!" he insisted. "You were strong enough. Why didn't you conquer them?"

She said: "We couldn't do that. We don't have any right to do that."

In that instant, it all became clear. Suddenly truth overwhelmed him, wave after wave, like a sickness. "No!" he cried. "No!" He dropped his head into his hands. "Lies," he murmured. "Lies, lies, lies!" He saw the wrongness, the terrible wrongness, and he searched desperately over his life for repudiation, an excuse. But he found none.

They had come to him and said, This is the law of life. And they took him and trained him, and showed him nothing else. He had been scarcely a child at the first school of soldiery, and they had fashioned his mind, a pliant mind, and ground doubts out (if there had been any). They told him that the law was strength, and strength was destiny, and destiny was to rule those below, obey those above, and destroy those who did not agree. There were no friends and enemies—only the rulers and the ruled. And the ruler must expand or die of admitted weakness.

"It's all lies!" he said. He felt the crumbling away of the certainty he had lived by. And before the helpless Oholo he felt weak and defeated and suddenly he realized that his mind shield was down.

She reached out gently to touch him.

Below, a police siren wailed in the streets. A car for corpses.

He tried to shake the hand away. "They lied," he said. "They lied about everything. They lied that you were ready to conquer us. They told us you were cowardly and

62

would kill us if we did not kill you first, and that we must take . . ."

She said: "It was worse than we thought. We did not think you were strong enough to attack us. Not here. We thought if we let you alone you would collapse of your own weight."

"I never knew," he said. "There wasn't any way to know. You have to do what everyone else does. You get to think they must be right." He made a small sound. "When I first came here—it started to bother me, when I saw the planet was unprotected—when I saw how strong you were . . . But I had so many things to do. I was too busy to think. But I felt something at the very first about your presence here . . ."

She stirred restlessly on the bed. He knew that he was defenseless before her because she had recovered, but she did not strike out. "Trying to help them," she said. "A few of us came to help them. They needed us. We were trying to prevent a war. And a few more years—if we'd . . . but that's gone now. You'll destroy it all."

He stood from the bed and it creaked.

"We were slowly changing their governments," she said. "We would have succeeded." He felt her mind slowly gather, and there was infinite bitterness, and he tensed. But still she did not strike at him.

"I want you to go," Parr said. "Before the other Knoug comes back. Get out."

Words damned up inside him. He had been trained to hate and trained to kill. The emotions were loose now. There was no outlet for them. He was frustrated and enraged. Hate bubbled about in him, fermenting. He had been trained to hate and to kill. Lauri winced as she felt the turmoil. "Get out!" he screamed.

The door crashed open.

Three figures lunged through.

"Lauri, thank God!" one of them cried. "We thought he'd killed you."

Parr suddenly found his arms held by two Oholos. "We got here as soon as we could pick up your thoughts."

Lauri said, "Jen is already dead."

One of the Oholos slapped Parr's face savagely. "We'll kill this one for that!" he snarled.

Lauri sprang from the bed and sent the weapon spinning from the hand of the leader of the three Oholos. He gave a startled gasp. The weapon hit the carpet and slammed to rest against the far wall. "Don't!" she cried.

"You're crazy!" the leader snarled. "What's wrong with you?"

"He saved my life," Lauri said, panting.

"He's Knoug," the leader sneered. "You know damned well he was trying to use you for something or other."

Parr stared, fascinated. He was surprised to find that he was not afraid. The shock of capture had not yet passed, and he seemed to be watching a drama from which he was removed.

"No!" Lauri said. "No, he wasn't!"

"How can you say that, Lauri? Look what he's done! Look what he's already done!"

"Unshield, Parr, show them," Lauri commanded.

Parr hesitated, trying to divine the plot and see what was required of him.

"It's a trick," the leader said. "They've got some way to fool us, even with an open mind!"

Lauri's eyes were wide.

The leader jerked his hand. "Kill him," he instructed.

The Oholo on Parr's left released Parr's arm and reached inside his coat for a weapon.

Lauri darted across the room and pounced on the weapon lying at the base of the wall. She seized it and rolled over. She aimed it steadily at the Oholo on Parr's left. "Don't do that," she said. "Let him go." She got to one knee.

Parr felt the grip ease on his right arm. He stood free. And for the rest time—with strange hope—the feeling of unreality vanished.

"You're insane!" the Oholo on Parr's right rasped.

She jerked the muzzle of the weapon. "I told you. He saved my life. He could have killed me. He didn't."

"A trick!"

"Get away from him!"

Reluctantly the two stood back, and the leader shifted uneasily on his feet.

"Don't you try it," Lauri suggested. "For all you know, I might really shoot. You aren't that quick."

Parr let out his breath.

"You!" she snapped at him. "Get to the door!"

Dazed, he obeyed her. He shook his head to clear it. He was afraid they would try to stop him.

"Open it!"

He opened the door and hesitated, looking at her.

"I'm coming," she snapped. Still covering the three Oholos she got to her feet and began to back toward him. "Don't follow," she warned the three before her.

"You know what this means?" the leader said. "You know what it means to help the enemy?"

"Go on out," she told Parr. "He saved my life," she said doggedly.

He obeyed. She followed him. She fumbled for the door knob, found it. "Run!" she cried. She slammed the door.

They ran desperately for the stairs. Their feet pounded on the soft carpet as they clattered down. She was almost abreast of him.

"Help me!" she cried when they passed the first landing.

And a moment later Parr knew what she meant. They were trying to tear into his mind, and she was holding them off with her own shield. He joined her as well as he could, marveling at the vast strength she had recovered.

"Hurry!" she cried. "I can't hold it much longer." She lurched into him and he put an arm around her waist.

And then they were through the lobby and into the silent street. No curious spectators were lingering to stare at the drying patch of dirty brown in the gutter beyond the awning.

"This way!" she cried.

As they fled on the pressure weakened. She was running fleetly at his side now, her brow unfurrowed, and yet he knew that she was still holding the shield under terrific pressure.

"In here," she gasped, suddenly turning into a narrow alleyway. "Stop!" she said. She half dragged him down to the pavement behind a row of packing crates.

"They'll be right after us!" he panted.

"No. Listen. Follow my lead. I think I can blanket us, if you help me."

Parr felt the warmth of her thoughts around him, and then they began to go up beyond his range and he had

65

to strain to stay with them. Underneath her thoughts his mind began to quiet, and, in a moment he felt—isolation.

"Help, here," she said.

He saw the weakness and strengthened it. With her helping, he found the range less high, and he could almost relax under it. And their minds were very close together, and their thoughts were completely alone. "We're safe here," she whispered.

He listened to his own far away breathing, and heard hers, too, softer but labored.

They crouched, waiting, and the street before them was quiet in the sunlight, for the mail trucks were out, and no taxis moved. The city—for the moment—was deathly still and waiting uneasily. The high air was sharp in his lungs.

"They've missed us," she said at length. "Wait! They're . . . They're after . . . it's another Knoug. They think we've separated, and they think it's you."

"That would be Kal," Parr said. "He must have been waiting nearby." He brought out the comset. "He must have seen us come out together."

He flicked open the comset, heard, ". . . joined with the Oholos. Parr and the other just left the hotel together."

"He's told the Advanceship," Parr said to the girl.

"It doesn't make any difference," Lauri replied wearily.

And Parr breathed a nervous sigh, for the hate had found its channel. The Empire had made him unclean and debased him, and he had to cleanse himself. His vast reserve of hate shrieked out against the Empire; their own weapon turned against them.

"I'd like to get back to the Advanceship," Parr said. "If I could get back, I could smash in their faces!"

"Oh," she said.

The comset sputtered excitedly. "Three Oholos after me! They're armed! Must be new ones. The other two weren't armed!"

The comset was silent.

"Three?" Parr said. "That's right, there were three. I thought there were just five on the whole planet.

"There's about fifty now. They landed last night. Out in the Arizona desert. They're the only ones who could get here in time."

Parr felt elation. But it passed. "Fifty . . . That's not enough to stop the invasion."

"It's all we could get here," Lauri repeated.

Parr groaned. "The Knougs will shield the planet tomorrow. It will trap those fifty on the surface. And us. They'll shoot us, if we're lucky. But I'd like to kill some first!"

The comset crackled, and the Shipvoice said: "How many new ones altogether?"

"I don't know," Kal answered. "I only know of three."

"We'll hurry the attack, then, before they're set. Can you hold out, Kal?"

"I don't know," Kal said.

The attack. The meaning of it suddenly rang in Parr's ears. Until a second ago, he had seen his hate as personal, and now he realized that the Empire was ready to capture a planet and then to destroy a System. And he saw the vast evil of the Empire hurtling toward Oholo civilization. He gnashed his teeth.

Lauri's hand jerked on Parr's elbow. "The one you call Kal is dead."

"I'm glad," Parr was grim. He remembered the savage eyes which the Earth disguise could not conceal. "I'm glad."

"Kal, Kal," the Advanceship called into emptiness. "Kal! Come in, advanceman Kal!"

Parr flipped off the comset.

She lowered the thought blanket completely. "Relax. Try to relax."

"Why did you do it?" he said. "Why didn't you let them kill me?"

"I don't know," she said slowly. "You saved my life. I couldn't let them kill you. I saw how you felt, how you suddenly changed. How you'd become a new person all at once. I couldn't pass judgment on you after that. I hated you and then I didn't hate you anymore. It doesn't matter. It's too late to matter. I . . . I . . ."

Her mind was warm against his.

"They're going back to join the others in the desert now," she said. "They're going to get ready to fight the attack."

"Lauri," Parr said. "Lauri, I've got to do something!"

67

10

(NEW YORK had broken windows now, and the streets were glass littered. An occasional white face peered out suspiciously from above a ground floor. But the heartbeat of subways was stilled. The cry had been: "You'll *starve* in the City!" and there had been an hysterical exodus, slow at first and then faster and faster and faster. The moon marched her train of shadows in the cavern streets.)

In Denver, the moon rode the mountains, calm, misted, serene.

"Parr," he spoke into the comset, and he felt Lauri's hand tighten on his elbow.

He glanced nervously at the sky. He was afraid to see the planet shield blossom as it might any minute to signify the attack had begun. But he feared even worse the absence of it.

"Parr?" the Advanceship spat back.

"The Oholos have a defense system around their own planets. *It won't do you any good to capture this one!* You won't be able to get nearer!"

"You are guilty of treason, Parr!"

"You can't get at their inner system! They have a defense ring that can blast your Fleet out of space."

"Lies!"

Parr glanced at Lauri beside him in the darkness. "No!" he said. "They are stronger than you are!"

"They would have attacked us if they were," the Knoug said calmly.

"They don't think like that!"

"A poor bluff, Parr."

"Stop!" Parr said, "Listen . . ." He looked at Lauri again. "No use. They cut off."

"I didn't think they'd bluff," Lauri said. She looked across the street. The street lights had come on on schedule, but they soon flickered out as the power supply waned. The city was dark.

"Will they scorch the planet?"

Parr glanced once more at the sky. "I think they're holding off trying to gain new information on your Oholos. Or maybe they're having trouble getting ready. We'll know very soon whether they'll scorch it or assault it with an occupation force."

Lauri said, "You tried."

"If we could *convince* them, like I was convinced . . . if we could show them you *were* strong and peaceful . . ."

"But we aren't strong, Parr. They caught us unprepared. If we had a year or two . . ."

"How long would it be before you could get reinforcements here?"

Lauri bit her lower lip. "At least a month. We'd have to organize the units and everything. No sooner."

"Oh."

"What were you thinking?"

"I thought," Parr said. " . . . I thought I might hold the attack off . . . for as much as a couple of hours."

"That wouldn't help."

Parr swallowed and cleared his throat nervously. "I don't know. Maybe it would give the Oholos more time to prepare. It might help a little."

"How?"

"I'm going to try that. I've got to do something, Lauri."

He flipped open the comset and started to speak, but the channel was already busy. It was filled with crackling explosive Knoug language.

Parr began to listen intently.

It was a conversation between the Flagship and one of the other ships of the Fleet. ". . . Parr's right," the other ship said. "So they're down there. They say they've fought Oholos, and he's probably right . . ."

"How many are there?" the Flagship demanded.

"Thirteen. All in the engine room."

"Tell them Parr was bluffing," the Flagship ordered.

"I already did."

"Tell them they're guilty of mutiny!"

"I did, and they still won't come out. They're the bunch that were in the assault at Coly. They've been hard to handle ever since."

"All right. Go after them with guns . . ."

What is it?" Lauri asked.

"Shhhh!" Parr cautioned.

69

A third circuit opened. "No other ship reports trouble. It's just this one bunch."

There was a harsh curse, gutteral and nasty. "These channels are open! The whole Fleet knows about that Coly bunch now!"

"What in hell! *God damn it, get them off!* We've got to isolate . . ." Click.

Parr stared at the cosmet in his hand.

Parr smiled thinly. "I did a little good, at least. A bunch of veterans must have been listening in on me . . . . One of the Fleet ships has a little trouble."

"Maybe . . .," she began excitedly.

"No," Parr said. "It was only thirteen Knougs. It's scarcely a ripple. It might make the rest of the Fleet a little uneasy—but they'll still take orders. I'm sorry Lauri, but it's not going to help much."

"How do you know it won't?" she insisted.

The bitter smile was still there. "I've seen something like it before. In five minutes it will all be over."

"Oh."

"Well," he said after a moment, "I better try to get the Ship. I'm going to hold them off as long as I can."

He clicked open the comset again. "Kal," he lied icily. "Advanceman Kal." For the first time he was glad of the tinny, voice disguising diaphragm.

"Get off!" the Advanceship ordered. "This is the Commander. We're under communication security, damn it!"

Parr nodded to himself in recognition of what had happened. Commanders were now on the whole communications network. It would prevent ordinary operators from spreading more news of mutiny through the Fleet; it would blanket the manufacturing of rumors. And, if things were running true to course the Flagship was monitoring all channels just in case.

"I've found out the Oholo's disposition," Parr hissed into the tiny comset. "Can you pick me up?"

There was a momentary pause.

". . . We thought you were dead, Kal. Why didn't you answer our calls?"

" . . . Broke my comset," Parr lied quickly. "I've just killed the traitor, Parr, and I'm using his."

There seemed to be suspended judgment in the Ship.

"If you pick me up, I can give you details. But you'll have to hurry! Two Oholos are closing in right now!"

"How many are there altogether?"

Parr hesitated. "Only twenty, Parr said. I think less than that. It won't be necessary to scorch the planet."

Again silence. Then the Flagship itself cut in, "All right. We'll pick you up. Where are you?"

"Denver." He made out the street signs in the darkness. "I'm here at a street corner. Eighteenth and Larimer."

"Someone who knows the territory from the Advance-ship can pick you up. Ten minutes. Hold on."

"Hurry!" Parr pleaded.

He cut off the comset. He realized he was frightened. The night was growing cold and he took two deep breaths. He let the comset slip from his fingers and shatter on the pavement. He kicked it away in savage annoyance, and snarled a curse.

Lauri shuddered inwardly at his violence, but he did not notice. And she forced a smile and touched him with a warm thought.

"I told them I was Kal," he said. "I . . . asked them to pick me up."

Lauri half gasped in surprise.

"They'll hold off the attack until they hear from me again. I'll try to keep them guessing as long as I can."

He was tired. He and Lauri had been walking the streets aimlessly for hours. At first there had been mobs after the mail delivery. Then the governor, conscious of what had happened in some Eastern cities, had declared martial law and only soldiers were supposed to be on the streets after sundown curfew. Already many people had fled the city in terror.

As he and Lauri walked side by side, Parr felt he had come to know her better than he had ever known anyone. He realized how strong his mind had grown under its month long test, and he knew that she had come to respect his strength, she who was so strong herself. But it was not her strength he respected. Strangely, it was her weak-ness—her compassion and her ability to forgive. An un-known thing, forgiveness, a beautiful thing.

She stood silently beside him. Then she said, "What time you gain won't matter."

"Maybe it will!" he said harshly, hating the Empire.

She stared into his face. She shook her head. "No," she said. She touched his cheek. "I ought to say something."

"What do you mean?"

"I don't know. That it's a brave thing you want to do . . ."

"After what I've done, I've got to do something to make up for my life."

"What you did doesn't matter anymore."

"Listen," he said. "Listen, Lauri. You better leave. Don't stand here any longer."

She did not move.

He gritted his teeth. "Hurry up!"

Her mind touched his gently, cloudlike, and drew away. "Let me go with you."

"You know that wouldn't work."

After a minute she turned reluctantly.

"Wait!" he cried after she had gone only a few steps. Eagerly she turned.

"Listen!" He glanced at his watch. "Listen. The Fleet is nervous. The Knougs are nervous. It might not take much after that Coly bunch revolted . . . They're yellow inside, and the seeds of doubt are there. If we could just make them believe you really had a weapon. An hour from now—give me *one hour*—you're to contact the Fleet on my comset and tell them the Oholos are going to destroy their Advanceship right before their eyes. Then tell them to get out, the whole Fleet, or you'll destroy every ship. That may make them think! That may make them believe!"

"But unless the Ship really is destroyed before their eyes . . ."

"I'll take it into hyperspace without a shield. One minute it will be there, the next minute it won't. Maybe they won't stop to figure it out."

"But you'll be killed!"

"Give me just one hour. Go on, damn it. Don't argue!" She seemed ready to cry. Then she bit her lip.

"But—Parr! Parr! I *can't!* How can I? *You broke the comset!*"

Parr's mind was dazed. He tried to think. ". . . Listen. Find the one Kal had! See if you can find that! You've *got to,* Lauri. It all depends on that. You've just got to find it!"

She hesitated.

"Don't argue," he insisted. "Hurry! They'll be after me any minute."

She seemed to want to say something.

"Run!" he cried. And then she was hurrying away and her mind left his entirely, so there would be no danger of detection when the scout ship came for him. And then she turned a corner, and was gone . . .

The silver saucer shaped scout ship zipped down the street, banked sharply and vanished, recording (Parr knew) electronic details for its mothership, the pick-up craft.

Parr waited, his mouth dry.

Finally—after what seemed a long time—he saw the dark, moving patch return. It lowered, and Parr could make out the details of the unlighted surface. He sighed with relief. Fortunately it was the small three passenger craft.

It hovered, closed on the intersection and settled. Hoping that neither of its crew knew him by sight, Parr sprinted from the shadows of the building to the opening door.

The distance seemed to unravel before his feet, lengthening like a magic carpet.

His feet hit the edge of the door almost together and grasping the sides he pulled himself in, falling forward and gasping for the crew's benefit, "Oholos!"

The inside of the craft, operating under low flying procedure, was darkened except for the dull orange of the instruments.

"Up!" Parr cried in Knoug, and the craft shot away pressing him to the floor even though the acceleration compensator was whirring in his ears.

He groaned and stiffened, anticipating the light when they were in second procedure level.

He heard one of the crew say: "Pick-up successful."

"Can you berth your craft on the Flagship?"

Parr felt a dread for he had thought to go to the Advanceship, and that was the one Lauri would name for destruction!

Relief came when the crewman said, "Wrong hanger sort. This isn't combat equipment, sorry."

"All right."

Parr breathed an easier sigh, and the communications set went off.

The lights came on.

Instinctively Parr lowered his head into his arms. He groaned again. "My leg," he mumbled.

"What?"

"Hurt my leg," he lied.

A crewman knelt beside him. Parr realized then that they were carrying an extra crewman.

The Knoug rolled him over.

There was a startled gasp of recognition and Parr hit him in the neck. He slumped down and Parr had to squirm from under his limp body.

"What the—!"

Parr was on his feet.

"That's not Kal!" one of the others said.

The pilot swiveled around.

Parr dove, realizing, even as he was in the air, that each Knoug was reaching for his focus gun.

He hit the standing Knoug. The Knoug teetered. Parr hit him again.

The pilot had his gun out.

Parr slammed a mental bolt at the pilot and he was surprised to see that the shield folded like hot butter. Even had he wished to he could not have stopped his assault from crisping the other's thoughts to oblivion. He was almost annoyed at the weakness.

He tried a mental assault at the other sagging crewman with equal results.

The craft started to spin out of control.

Parr struggled forward, was slammed sideways, and far below he could see moonlight flash on water.

He was thrown into the controls on the second spin, and he pulled back the emergency equalizer in desperation. The craft skittered.

And then he was in control.

He found the beam on the dial. He was to the left. He centered on it and followed it in.

He jockeyed below the gaping hatch of the Advance-ship and came up slowly. The controls were stiff. It was a ticklish job.

Then he was inside. He shied left to set the craft down.

It bounced and half rolled on the deck. Then he struggled to the door.

When he opened it there was an orderly waiting. "That was a hell of a landing," he said. "For—hey!"

He went down easily under the assault. Parr realized his mind had grown even stronger than he had supposed. For the first time he began to hope that he really stood a chance of making it.

He glanced at his watch.

Almost forty-five minutes! It had seemed only five . . .

Lauri ran toward the second building. Her mind usually smooth and calm, was now a welter of conflicting thoughts. She had tried to reach the other Oholos. But they shut themselves off. No help from them.

There were no cabs out. And the telephones were dead. She was desperately afraid Kal was in the morgue but she could not risk the time to be sure. Vaguely she remembered the siren that had squalled when the police came for the body of the Oholo and his Earth assailant who had been killed outside the hotel. But she could not remember another siren near the time Kal had been killed. She was forced to assume the police had not come for him.

But she could not be sure.

If the police had not come, she reasoned, then he had not been killed before witnesses. Therefore he had not been killed in the streets.

She knew that he had seen them leave the hotel. That narrowed the range. That he had been killed shortly afterward by the Oholos narrowed the range even more.

He had not been moving when he was killed, and he had just finished reporting Parr's and her flight, meaning that he had been stationary since his observation. And there would be no reason for the Oholos to move or to hide the body.

Therefore his body should be where it had fallen.

There had been four business buildings in the vicinity where a man could have been killed unseen.

She pushed open the doors to the second. The ground floor, within observation range, was easily checked. So was the second. Third. Fourth. Fifth.

She was back in the street. Two more buildings. Half

75

her time gone. She glanced at her watch for verification. Each of the two remaining buildings had four floors.

The nearest one was locked. But there was a light inside. She was puzzled. Then she saw the cleaning maid come down the front stairs, carrying a brace of candles in one hand and a mop and bucket in the other. The old woman moved slowly, unconcerned, oblivious of the outside world, intent only on her job. Lauri shuddered, but she knew that the face would not be calm if she had seen a corpse in her duties. Therefore, there was no corpse inside.

One building left!

But a few minutes later she was back in the streets. There had been nothing on the lower floor, the second floor, and the two top floors needed only a glance.

She sobbed desperately.

Something had been wrong with her reasoning, and she had only twenty minutes left to start from the beginning and find the Knoug's body.

Parr ran quickly along the corridor. He passed two incurious Knougs. He continued on, winding upward toward the control room which he had to capture. There would be a delicate balance of timing and luck between success and failure.

He was not frightened now, even though he knew he could not personally win the fight in capture or success. His mind was calm. Strangely, too, it was at peace.

He clambered up the final ladder, his hands unsteady on the rungs. The control room door was closed. He tensed, listening, wondering how many of the enemy were inside.

He knocked, his knuckles brittle on steel. He thought, in that fleet second, of Lauri. He wondered dimly if she had found the comset.

"Yeah?"

"I've got Kal out here, sir!" Parr said briskly, hoping to imitate the orderly's voice.

"What the hell!" a voice from inside roared, "I thought we told you to take him down to the Commander's office."

Parr held his breath.

He heard an indistinct mutter of voices inside and he

knew that one of them must be on the inter-phone to the Commander.

"Something screwy here!" the voice roared indignantly.

Parr hit the door and it crashed inward with an echoing clang.

He catapulted into the congested control room. In a glance he saw there were only two Knougs. One was at the control banks, half turned in surprise. The other held the phone limply in his left hand, his eyes staring.

Parr kicked the door shut viciously and the sound rang in his ears. He launched himself at the Knoug with the phone. He felt his head meet a soft stomach and he heard explosive air pop from the man's lungs. The Knoug went over backwards, down hard.

The other one roared an oath.

Parr walked on the fallen one's face. He stomped the face and it gurgled. He stomped again in fury as all his frustration and new bitterness found an outlet. He locked the other Knoug in mental battle, but the mind he met was strong, catching him off guard.

The Knoug dove for the huge comset to warn the Fleet.

Parr could hear, from the receiver of the dangling phone, the Commander saying over and over again, "What the hell's going on? What the hell's going on?"

Parr brought the remaining Knoug to his knees with a mental assault.

Parr backed toward the door. As he fought mentally, he managed to slide the force bar across it. They'd play hell getting him out, at least.

His enemy was down, quivering. Parr panted desperately, and then from beyond the door, he felt the growth of mental assault force. Three minds hurrying toward him! Two more minds came in and he staggered and almost fell.

Then he was down, as if from a hammer blow to the chin. He fought, sickened. He began to crawl toward the control board. And fighting, he struggled up, as if under a great weight. New minds came in. And still he could fight. But he was almost down again.

(Five minutes, he thought.)

He found the right lever, pulled.

There was the crackle of the heterodyne mind shield. And the control room was isolated by a high, shrill whine.

77

He winced, recovering, and smiled inwardly at the careful devices Knoug officers had to protect themselves against a mutinous crew.

He dampened all the thrust engines with three hacking strokes at knife switches, being careful to get the right ones. He ripped out the engine room control. The Advanceship was dead in space for at least an hour.

He staggered to the comset. He stumbled over the dead Knoug and kicked the body. He shattered the transmitter with a furious blow.

With fumbling fingers he ripped away the seal the Commander had placed on the receiver. He snapped the volume control to the right. The radio whined.

Someone was trying to call the Advanceship, and Parr smiled grimly.

Another circuit broke in on the call. "Their commander is questioning the advancemen they brought up, I imagine. Let him go. The information we got from the Texas advanceman supercedes it anyway."

Parr cursed monotonously.

"Forward bank in!" another circuit reported.

"Nine stations on planet shield. Ready?"

There was a crackling of readiness.

"We'll hit before it. Try to get it set in fifteen minutes."

"In position, there. Eight, back a little."

"Clear hulls. Unscreen."

"Check . . . Check . . ."

Parr glanced at his watch. The hour had only minutes of life. What was wrong with Lauri?

"Ready around?"

The Fleet was getting ready to move. Parr screamed in wild frustration.

At the door, the force field was beginning to show strain. Outside they had a huge force director focused on it. Parr speculated idly how they had managed to get it up from the engine room so quickly. The force field at the door began to peel. In a few minutes it would shatter and the control room would be an inferno with every switch and bit of metal melted into smoking blobs.

She was searching the shops, kicking in glass, when necessary to gain entrance. She was listening, now, and time dribbled away. Standing amid broken glass, she

78

cocked her head hoping to hear the whisper of the still active comset.

Ten minutes.

What had been wrong with her logic? Why hadn't Kal's body been in one of the four buildings? Even as she searched on she reviewed it in her mind, until suddenly, with an abrupt snap she knew that she had overlooked one. There were not four possible buildings but five.

Kal might have been hiding in the hotel itself!

Nine minutes.

And how many front rooms were in the hotel? A twelve storied welter of windows, and he might be behind any one.

Nine minutes.

Automatically she was running for the hotel.

(Not the lower floors, she thought, or the Oholos would have had him sooner. They must have come down and then gone back up or else the whole time element was wrong.)

One of the upper floors then?

She would have to chance that.

She was in the deserted lobby. As she ran across it she marveled at the panic of a few hours ago. She saw a busy looter in the shadows, and there were not, certainly enough soldiers to be everywhere.

In her headlong rush she did not see the human form on the second landing before she crashed into him. She gasped as the breath went out of her lungs.

The man reached out for her. "What happened?" His voice was desperate. "I've been asleep, and all of a sudden, when I wake up—"

"Let me go!"

"What happened?" he said pathetically. "The city's so *still*."

She pushed him back and continued up the stairs.

He ran after her. "Wait!"

At the top floor she saw no exit to the roof.

The corridor was "U" shaped, the bottom of the "U" facing onto the street. Six rooms on it.

"Young lady!" the man cried, rounding the corner of the stairs below her. She dropped her mental range into a low register and struck toward him. But she could not quite find his range and he shook his head and continued up the stairs. She waited, and when he arrived, she said, "Sorry," and hit him on the chin. He rolled halfway down the short flight of stairs.

She searched the six rooms. All were unlocked and empty, and the doors slammed in her wake.

Nothing.

She gritted her teeth and headed for the stairs and the next floor below.

Parr shattered the glass from the emergency deep space suit. He ripped the suit from the hangar and struggled into it with anxious fingers.

He hesitated, holding the helmet in his hands.

The force field at the door was nearly gone. The radio crackled with Knoug attack orders.

And then—with infinite relief—he heard her voice, crackling over the other voices. She sounded short of breath and excited.

"What's that?" someone roared in Knoug, and Parr realized they did not understand English, the common language they had used on the planet.

"Idiots!" Parr shrieked. "Fools! Can't *any* of you understand!"

"I'm going to destroy your Advanceship," Lauri said breathlessly. "I am an Oholo. I'm . . ."

Suddenly a Knoug was translating her message.

Last minute instructions to the Fleet ceased.

"I'm going to destroy your Advanceship," she said again. And then, after a breath, she said, "Be careful! Be careful!" And he knew that the last was not to them but to him.

He could wait no longer. The force field was seconds thin. His mind cried desperately, "Hurry!" He clamped down the helmet and all sound vanished.

But her words rang in his mind, "Be careful!" and he was grateful for them. They choked in his throat.

Then he threw the Advanceship into hyperspace.

There was a pinwheel of motion that slammed him into the control panel. He could not hear, but everywhere, around him, metal screamed and wrenched and tore.

The force director beyond the door spun loose and sprayed the Knougs around it, and they vanished. It jerked its current cable and was still. A vast rent in the hull let the air whoosh out into hyperspace, and the Knougs all over the Ship puffed and exploded.

Parr came slowly to his senses. He staggered direction-less around the control room. Everything was a shambles.

After a while—nearly an hour had elapsed—he was wandering through silent corridors. It was hot inside his suit.

He found the pick-up ships eventually, but they were ripped from their moorings. One seemed upright and serviceable. He tested the motor. The motor worked. He got out and struggled with the escape hatch. Finally it came loose.

He taxied the pick-up ship out of the mother ship.

Hyperspace was grey and hideous. Here and there lights flashed. The vast, battered derelict of the Advance-ship lay below him. Hyperspace spread away. He blasted further from the gutted hull and brought up the space shield of his craft. It wavered around him. Behind him the tortured Advanceship exploded.

He hit back toward real space. The craft skittered under his hands as he wrenched at the controls. The motor was strong, but its delicate shielding apparatus had been dam-aged and there was a sickening jolt. The shield was off and Parr was falling, down, down, down, and lights in his head exploded.

And he thought it was infinitely sad that he had done something decent for the first time and now he was to be punished for all the rest. Then he knew no more . . .

The comset had erupted into a babble of incredible confusion after her message. She waited leadenly. She warned the Fleet once more. "If you do not leave at once, we Oholos will destroy your whole Fleet." She had no way of knowing what was happening.

The Knoug commanders, unnerved, cried among them-selves:

"No weapon I ever heard of could do *that!*"

"The advanceman was right! They can destroy us!"

"I say we don't stand a chance!"

"Did you hear? It just *vanished.*"

"I'm going to order my ship back."

"I've already shielded for hyperspace."

"What's the Flagship say?"

"What's the Flagship *say?*"

"Commander Cei just pulled out. That makes five."

"As for me, I say, Let's go!"

"The Flagship has already got its hyperspace shield turned on!"

Slowly the voices died away. The comset was silent in Lauri's hand, and she knew that the Fleet had gone. The Advanceship was destroyed.

Remembering Parr, she bowed her head. She saw the body of Kal lying at her feet, where she had found it in the second room on the tenth floor. And she was crying without sound.

II

SHE FINALLY got through to the other Oholos. They listened, because the expected attack had not come.

They came for her and she met their airship in the street. They soared above the silent city of Denver.

"A Knoug!" one said. "Who ever would have thought a *Knoug* would do that!"

She tried to explain but they did not listen for they were busy with other thoughts. She was still crying, but inwardly now. She said, "Don't you see what he might have *become* within a few years?"

"Imagine hitting hyperspace without a shield," one Oholo said.

"It must have turned the ship inside out!"

"So the Knougs actually believed it was a weapon that did it!" another said, pleased.

Lauri said, woodenly, "He was very strong. He was almost as strong as I am. He would have become even stronger."

"There's no Knoug as strong as one of our best workers, Lauri."

"He was more than a Knoug," she insisted gently. "A Knoug would have just—just gone on being what he was."

She fell silent, remembering.

"It played hell with this planet," an Oholo said. "It'll take years to straighten it out."

"Not years," another said, looking down at the night. "No. I think not years. One of the governments we were primarily concerned with has been changed. The people finally got the chance to overthrow it, and they did. That's a good sign. I think our work will be easier now. It's always easier to rebuild than to change."

Lauri!

She froze. "Listen!"

And they listened, high up.

Lauri!

"Yes!" she cried.

Come to me!

She rushed to the pilot room. She took the controls and spun the ship.

"Did you hear that?" an Oholo said, awed.

"Yes, said another. " . . . He not only went in unshielded, but he managed to get back!"

They shook their heads.

And within fifteen minutes she had found his ship, lying below in dying moonlight.

She brought the aircraft down and within seconds she was running to the wreckage and pulling his limp body from it.

When the space helmet was off his head, he gasped, "Tore hell out of my big ship. And . . . then I even . . . up and . . . wrecked this one, landing . . . I'm just . . . damned clumsy."

"Get the surgeon!" Lauri cried.

She held his head in her arms while her lips moved soundlessly. Then she bent to kiss him on the mouth after the Earth fashion, and Parr had never experienced such a sensation of trust and surrender and promise. He let his hand move gently down her arm.

"We'll stay here," she whispered. "We'll stay here and help these Earth people, you and I. You'd like that? To help them?"

"Yes," he said. "It would be nice to . . . build instead of destroy. It would be nice, I think. You and I could help them. I'd like that."

The surgeon came, and they took Parr out of the suit and after a while the surgeon said, "I don't know much about Knougs. But I'm glad this one is going to be all right."

Lauri laughed hysterically. The tears were open again. *"I* couldn't kill him," she sobbed.

The other Oholos looked puzzled and polite.

"It's a joke!" she said, dizzy with relief. "Of course he'll live, because even I couldn't kill him!"

Parr smiled up at her.

THE END

STAR GLADIATOR

By Dave Van Arnam

1 Flames at Midnight

IT WAS MIDNIGHT in the capital city of Kallor when the Star Guards of Zarmith II struck the planet Kalvar.

Telvar Gri and his wife Eila were hosting a fellow member of the Grand Council, the widower Alhavan Tor, and his two young daughters. The shimmering blue of Alhavan's cape contrasted with the dark grey of Telvar's.

A breeze had sprung up; the light curtains entwined in the gigantic neo-oak danced with a soft jingling noise.

They were seated near the edge of Telvar's roof garden, on the fifth floor of his mansion which overlooked the tree-lined Avenue of Vega, wide and stately, leading to the Tower of the Grand Council some seven blocks away. The entire mansion was built surrounding the huge neo-oak so that the spendid crown of the tree spread majestically just over their heads.

The meal rituals were about to begin, and Telvar's son, Jonnath, itched in the prescribed shirt of plant fibers. Telvar looked at him with some impatience; it was time to prepare the food.

Jonnath stood. His close-cropped black hair added emphasis to his strong face. At fifteen, he had not reached his full growth of seven to eight feet, but at six feet he towered over eleven year old Triez, who had not begun the hereditary Kalvaran spurt. Sheira, fourteen, was almost as tall as he. The fleeting thought touched Jonnath's mind that she was almost old enough for their parents to begin marriage bargaining. He felt a certain warmth of enthusiasm at the thought.

He strode to the Proving table, where the food was set out ready for the riutals. Then he turned; he now had the right to break into any conversation.

But they had fallen silent, waiting for him. Triez's hair, as black as Darkside and long to her waist, rippled gently in the breeze. Sheira tossed her short golden hair briefly and stood up herself. Alhavan had permitted her and Triez to serve in the guest rituals; she was obviously nervous, since she'd gotten to her feet before she should have.

Jonnath reached into the plain bowl in the center of the Proving table, and drew out a small clod of dirt.

"Lest we forget the soil of Earth," he said formally, and rubbed the dirt between his hands, careful to let it fall back into the small bowl. Jonnath marveled once again that though the dirt was really from their garden, the symbolism reached him emotionally.

He started to put his hands in the vibraclean, but remembered in time to use the small pitcher of water instead.

Drying his hands on a towel, he continued.

"Men of Earth, we are not of Earth. Our land is alien and our skies are new. Look upward, and do not forget." All looked up, where the bright spangle of the Ten-Star Complex glittered above them with quiet familiarity.

The main course that night was steak; Jonnath started to pick up the fire knife for hallowing, but caught Telvar's sharp glance in time.

As Jonnath flicked its switch, the multiwave tuner throbbed and jangled with the hieretic music of Ziaphar, empire city of the Ten Systems a hundred lightyears distant, though what they heard was actually retransmitted in Kallor Wave Central.

He continued the ritual: "Conquerors of the stars, we are only human. Where we choose to set our feet, that land is ours; yet we are aliens. The shores of space do not protect us; we protect ourselves."

Then he picked up the fire knife. Since there were

two serving in the guest rituals, he cut off two small shreds of raw meat and set them above the flame of the small wood fire in the brazier that stood by the Proving table.

The aroma of cooking flesh and wood smoke had always struck him as rather unpleasant, he realized, as he took the remainder of the meat to the clean bare metal surface of the sonic stove.

He was youthfully impatient for the rigmarole to be over. He knew Telvar Gri made much out of keeping the rituals meaningful. His friend Jarley Lar's father always kept it simple, a few stock sentences and the servants to perform all the tedious rituals and Questioning.

He wanted to sonocook the steak, eat it, and get the whole thing over with. There was the autoclang that had come that afternoon; he'd only had a moment before the meal to show it off to Sheira, and Triez. The clattering popular tunes of a thousand planets awaited them downstairs, and they had to listen to droning, bell-punctuated priest music.

The two bits of fire-cooked meat were done. He carried them to the dinner table, and Triez stood up beside her sister.

"That we do not become prisoners of civilization and technology, we must remember the guestly ways of our ancestors," Jonnath said, and the girls took the pieces of meat with their hands.

"Fire is still fire," said Sheira, and ate the burned morsel.

"We are never helpless if we do not forget," said Triez, completing the ritual phrases and eating the meat.

"Well, then," said Telvar Gri, sitting back in his chair, "I think we can have the Questions while we wait, don't you, Eila?"

Eila nodded with a smile, and Alhavan Tor cleared his throat.

"Frankly, Telvar," Alhavan said, grinning, "I'm so starved I could eat a whole bisfas. I know you look down on having the Rituals performed by the servants, but do you really think all this is still necessary?"

Telvar smiled quietly. "At least for special occasions, my friend," he said.

Alhavan made a mocking groan, and Jonnath sighed to himself as he flicked on the sonostove, paused a moment while the steak cooked, then flicked it off. The girls came over to help him serve.

"Telvar," said Alhavan, "I know you'd like to keep this for your precious Questions, but look at that! Five years ago it took a solid thirty seconds to cook a slab of steak and now it's only four seconds. That's *progress*, man! What makes you think we'll ever need to cook with fire again? Doesn't even taste good that way, with all that wood-smoke flavor. I know, I know," he added, seeing Telvar about to protest, "if anything *should* happen. . ."

They all began eating; after a few minutes, Telvar spoke. "Jonnath, why do we continue the Vegan Rituals?"

"Survival, Father," said Jonnath, swallowing a piece of meat hastily and knowing Telvar wouldn't be satisfied with the answer.

"Come, Jonnath, survival is more than a piece of fire-blackened meat," Telvar chided.

"Very well. Survival is not in the ritual, it is in the reality." He thought for a moment. "We must understand reality. The sonostove is part of reality, that of the science of the race. But fire is the reality behind the science; science may fail us, fire never will."

Telvar looked stern. "The phrases are yours, but they merely echo the tradition."

Jonnath thought Jarley Lar didn't know how lucky he was; Telvar was never satisfied with the traditional answers.

He tried again. "The Rituals remind us of the tradition, and the tradition reminds us of reality." Then he saw the way. "But it is the ritual of Answer and Question that give it meaning. Without that, the Rituals are simply ceremony."

"Mmmm," said Telvar. "Well, then, 'What did you learn in school today?'"

Jonnath suppressed an urge to show his irritation. Was his father trying to humiliate him? That was a question for a child, for someone like Triez. Telvar hadn't asked that since Jonnath was twelve, and besides, Telvar knew the answer, since the two of them had spent the day reviewing Gallen's *Notes On Recent Galactic History*.

Then again he saw the way. "That you think Kalvan is

getting soft, and has been for two hundred years." He paused to think before continuing, and was surprised when his father interrupted him.

"Yes," said Telvar, "I saw the first signs when I was little more than your age. Alhavan remembers. . ."

"I do that," boomed Alhavan, worrying a piece of gristle that had lodged in his teeth. "Dom, but you've been propagandizing me ever since! By Phanoc—"

Telvar smiled, a little wearily. "And you agree with me now, don't you?"

"Well, yes, of course," Alhavan said, removing the piece of gristle from his mouth and depositing it on the side of his plate. "Cursed little we can do about it any more, though."

"For twenty years and more we've been ignored by the Grand Council. Kalvar maintained its independence in the old expansionist era of the Zia Complex, they say, and with the Ten Systems grown decadent we have nothing to fear." Telvar sighed. "But there are newer empires growing. Zarmith II feeds their bloody Star Games by their conquests, and one day they will grow eager to sack Ziaphar itself—and we lie between."

He shook his head. "One planet cannot stand alone . . ."

Jonnath had heard it many times; he didn't really care. The ins and outs of galactic history to him seemed irrelevant. No one would want Kalvar; its two-g's-Standard gravity was quite unpleasant for visitors. Their Vegan ancestors, one of the earliest colonial groups from Earth after the invention of the multiwave drive, had turned this into a double advantage through selective breeding, and Kalvaran had become magnificent physical specimens, splendidly efficient fighters. In the past they had fought marauding raiders off countless times, had fought the Ten Systems itself to a standstill; they were unique. They did not fear the incompetent Emperor Shaikon III of the Ten Stars, nor anyone else.

Jonnath listened as his father argued, but did not join in. He was more interested in after the meal. He was sure now that Alhavan was eager to discuss marriage terms with Telvar and Eila.

He looked at Sheira, and was startled to realize she had been watching him.

Shyly her eyes dropped away, then turned back to him. He was surprised to realize that she was blushing; she'd never done that before.

Did she also suspect her father's purpose?

"You're blushing!" whispered Triez in his ear.

Telvar Gri glanced sharply at them; Jonnath felt the confusion on his face—duplicated on Sheira's. Triez looked slightly smug.

Telvar cleared his throat. "There seem to be undercurrents here that are not directly related to the main stream of galactic history," he said dryly, and Alhavan chuckled appreciatively.

"Didn't know any Esper genes had gotten into this quadrant, Telvar!" Alhavan said.

Jonnath flushed again; so it was true! He was glad it was to be Sheira; he'd always rather liked her, as girls went—and she did not seem to be unhappy at the whole idea.

Telvar's face assumed a more formal set once more. *More ritual*, thought Jonnath. *Can't he be more human at times like these?*

"I'm sure your daughters excel at the guest rituals of meal ending, Alhavan; but it seems to me that we might well forgo Vegan customs long enough for one more native to Kalvar, eh?"

Alhavan positively beamed. "I have waited for this conversation for many years, as you know, Telvar."

"Then, children, may I request you withdraw? We wish to speak in private." Telvar's tone was warm despite the characteristic formality of his words.

Jonnath allowed Sheira and Triez to rise first, as was the custom, then got to his feet.

"We haven't had a chance to really hear the new autoclang, Shiera, Triez; shall we go downstairs?" Jonnath groaned to himself; he sounded as bad as his father now!

They had reached the wooden stairs that wrapped in a downward spiral around the neo-oak, when something like a huge lightning-bolt flashed through the sky.

It was followed by the slapping boom of a tremendous explosion.

The multiwave tuner gave a "blat" and fell to hissing quietly . . .

Jonnath stood poised in shock at the edge of the stair-well.

A series of explosions rocked the entire city, and the skyline of Kallor was lit with the flames of dozens of huge fires.

"Invasion! Father—you were right!" Jonnath was startled to hear his own voice.

Then Triez dashed to her father, sobbing hysterically.

Sheira grasped Jonnath's arm, and whispered, almost tonelessly, "What is it? What is it? What is it?"

His mother was gesturing to him, a stricken look on her pale face. He drew Sheira with him; Eila embraced them both as she wept.

"There is no honor in being a prophet," whispered Telvar Gri. He had not risen, but sat gripping the sides of his chair as he stared at the flames rising ever higher.

"Do you have arms and shelter in your home?" asked Alhavan quietly.

"Brun hand rifles—what use are they against those cursed new forceshields of patterned electricity? Oh, and Kreshagar swords," Telvar added bitterly, "for ceremonial dueling, though they're not toys. No, I've nothing to fight them with, nor do I think there are weapons strong enough on the whole planet. I suppose I should have arranged for shelter, but it has always seemed to me that if it did come to that, shelter would be as useless as weapons."

"Are you so sure, then, that Zarmith II has sent the Star Guards?" Alhavan still spoke quietly, soothing Triez by stroking her long black hair. The girl's sobs lessened.

Telvar shrugged. "Who else? Shaikon and the Ten Stars certainly haven't such power—or the will."

The multiwave tuner suddenly jolted everyone with a siren blast.

"The emergency override circuit!" said Alhavan. "Now at least we can find out what's being done!"

A voice came over the tuner. "Planetary emergency override. This is Deputy Leader Visrak Hon speaking from the Tower of the Grand Council."

Instinctively they all looked down the Avenue of Vega to the Tower. A vague yellow shimmering now quivered around the entire vast structure, and darting shapes of small space pursuit craft were flitting about it.

The Deputy Leader continued talking, his voice calm amid the sights and sounds of chaos. "All major cities are under attack. The Grand Council wishes everyone to take shelter and to keep calm. We have not yet heard from all military establishments, but reports so far indicate our men are holding their own. We are—" Another voice interrupted, speaking indistinctly offmike.

"It has just been reported . . . it has been verified that the attackers are Star Guards. Attempts are now being made to contact Zarmith II by multiwave. It is hoped that negotiations with . . ."

The voice faded under, but continued to talk in reassuring tones, while another voice came on, an old voice, a tired voice.

"Senior Councillor Darzal here, speaking only through Council tuners. Let me be honest with you, my friends. We do not have a chance."

"But the shield, man, the shield!" Alhavan stood at the edge of the roof now, and slammed his fist against the neo-oak railing. "It *must* hold!"

The Senior Councillor continued, over the reassuring drone of his Deputy Leader. "If we'd had a few more years to work on the theory, we might have done something with the forcefield. But as it is, the shield is not going to last."

From high above the Tower of the Grand Council a great beam flashed downward and struck the yellow shimmering that was the shield. A bright flare of light sprang up and the shimmering became fainter; but then the beam winked out.

"Can't take many of those," the voice said, sounding more distant. "But we're helpless. Visrak will continue calming the public as long as we hold out. I've directed the installations at Jornagar to carry on after we go. Over a thousand ships struck us. No warning, of course, and the multiwave drive is indetectable. Must be three-quarters of a million men, and most of them with the new forcefields." He paused.

"Curse you, Telvar," came the Senior Councillor's voice wearily, "you were right. And now they've ringed the city. They're marching inward, killing or capturing everyone, everyone who resists, and their families . . ."

"I could have tried harder . . ." whispered Telvar; he

92

seemed to shrink into himself. "Harder . . ."

There was another crackle from the multiwave tuner. "Well . . ." said the Senior Councillor, then stopped for a moment, as if it were impossible to speak what must be spoken.

Then—"Jornagar has been obliterated. That was our only hope. They're everywhere now, and they're wrecking everything . . ."

From above the Tower they saw the great beam flash again. This time it was the yellow shimmering that winked out first.

For an anticlimatic moment, nothing at all happened further. Then there was a distant "whoosh" as something flashed through the sky downward at the now unprotected Tower.

The missile struck.

The Tower shuddered for an instant, then blew apart with a shattering roar.

A tremendous gout of flame swept skyward; Jonnath felt the heat of it.

The multiwave tuner was silent once more . . .

Jonnath placed his hand on his father's shoulder. Slowly Telvar covered it with his own. They did not look at each other.

2 "A World Dies Tonight!"

SOME OF IT they saw from the roof-garden, much of it Jonnath pieced together later.

It was a night of thunder and blood and flames for Kallor. In their forcefields of patterned electricity that shimmered crimson, the Star Guards moved like weird shapes of flame thrugh the starlit night, among the towering buildings and along the wide and pleasant avenues.

Elite Death Patrols clad in black moved with the Star Guards, armed with the Nangee flashers that could not be carried in the patterned fields. The Nangees wreaked their blinding havoc while the Star Guards themselves, armed with their incongruous swords and slow-firing Sefpan airpistols, literally cut through the Kalvaran.

The Kalvaran were helpless, armed with useless Brun pistols and light rifles for the most part, which fired explosive pellets which could not penetrate the crimson fields.

Now the Star Guards were advancing down the Avenue of Vega. Knots of men set up defensive positions, block by block—and block by block the Star Guards moved forward relentlessly, reached the positions, and hacked the defenders to pieces.

Then the Death Patrols moved in, beamed the Kalvaran wounded with Nangee flashers, and held the survivors prisoner with snake ropes.

On the roof top, they watched in silent horror-filled shock, unable to talk, to cry, to flee—only to watch as the Star Guards brought terror and death and destruction to their city.

Then Telvar sprang to his feet. A low buzzing sounded in the air, growing nearer, and at the same time the building across the avenue burst into sudden flame.

Everyone on the roof could see them clearly now—a half-dozen Star Guards approaching them on flying sleds.

Six Star Guards in their bloody shimmering force-fields—and another clad only in solid black.

"Of course," said Telvar hurriedly. "They want the Council—there's probably another detachment at your home by now, Alhavan; they'll want all of us."

Alhavan nodded and said, "If we all run, they'll get us all. You and I, we'll stay; they should be satisfied with two of us at once."

"No!" said Eila, speaking for the first time. "I shall stay also, Telvar. It will give the children even more of a chance."

"No time to argue," said Alhavan over Telvar's protests. "Only moments before they see how many are here!"

"Very well," said Telvar. "Down the stairs with the girls, Jonnath—*now*."

Jonnath's training took over from his numbed mind; he would have stayed with his father and mother, but there was his training—and there were the girls.

He grabbed Sheira's hand and pushed Triez forward. The buzzing of the flying sleds grew rapidly louder as the three youngsters dashed for the wooden stairs leading down around the neo-oak.

They were barely out of sight when the seven plat-forms landed with a series of loud clangs.

Sheira stumbled and fell down the last few steps to the fourth floor landing, but the noise from the sleds masked the sound.

She attempted to get to her feet, winced, and grabbed her ankle.

Jonnath helped her up and they started for the next flight of stairs. But the sound of strange voices on the roof garden stopped him.

"You are Grand Councilman Telvar Gri?" a harsh voice asked accusingly.

Jonnath could picture the contemptuous look on his father's face as he did not deign to reply.

"You're in luck," came Alhavan's voice, muffled through the stairwell. "I'm also a Grand Councilman—Alhavan Tor. *At* your service, I'm sure." His tone was icy.

Triez began to sob again; Sheira gave her a light slap across the lips and the girl made a tiny noise of surprise. And stopped sobbing.

"Splendid," said the menacing voice, "we were going to . . . visit you next. Lieutenant."

The three downstairs heard another voice say, "Yes, sir?"

"Beam them."

Triez let out a low moan of comprehension, and Sheira turned a blind stricken face to Jonnath; soundless tears rolled down her cheeks.

"I'm—I'm—" Triez started to choke out another sob; Jonnath held both girls tightly, protectively, in his arms.

His own face was expressionless, in his intense concentration on what was happening just above them—and on controlling himself, preventing himself from dashing up the winding stairs in a futile attempt to do . . . what? No, it was important to protect the girls if they were to have any chance at all.

There was nothing else he could do.

There was a sizzling "snap" from above—the Nangee flashers, Jonnath knew—and a woman's scream. Then two more "snaps" in rapid succession . . . and silence.

"Weren't there children, Captain?" came a voice.

Jonnath released Triez and started once more to help

95

Sheira down the next flight of stairs. But the captain's next words stopped him.

"We'll lob a beta grenade in the front door, Lieutenant," said the harsh voice. "That will take out the whole building."

"Yes, sir."

The humming buzz began again; it sounded curiously louder to Jonnath now. Then the squad was lifting upward on the sleds.

Triez burst into uncontrolled wails of anguish, as Sheira tried to speak through her own tears. "Are . . . are they dead?"

Jonnath nodded. He could not speak for a moment as he tried hard to quell his own grief . . . and succeeeded.

"Beta grenade!" he said suddenly.

Sheira stared at him as he grabbed them and darted into action.

"Upstairs, quickly! The tree—our only chance!" It was a hair-thin chance, he knew; there could be only seconds before the flying sleds descended all the way to the street, only seconds for setting the timer on the beta grenade.

And perhaps ten more seconds for the squad to get away.

Nine.

He thrust Triez up the stairs ahead of him, braced Sheira, started to climb himself.

Eight.

Sheira broke away and began running up the stairs despite the pain in her leg.

Seven.

Triez was almost at the top of the stairs.

Six.

"Into the branches, Triez!" Jonnath shouted, aware of the smothered groan of pain from Sheira ahead of him, every time she put her weight on her injured ankle.

Five.

Triez was scrambling into the thick branches of the immense crown of the gigantic tree; Sheira was at the head of the stairs, unable to stand the pain in her ankle any more.

Four.

Jonnath was at the head of the stairs catching up Sheira in his arms and running for the nearest low branch.

Three.

Sheira waited, holding her balance on one foot, as Jonnath hoisted himself into the tree.

Two.

Jonnath reached down and started to hoist Sheira after him into the branches. *No time to see their parents lying there,* he thought, *and thank Phanoc for that, at least, for the girls' sakes.*

One.

Sheira was beside him in the branches, scrambling along a thick limb to the crotch where it met the huge bole of the living tree.

There was a timeless pause. An extra second . . . two . . . three . . .

The beta grenade went off with a boom that tore the building apart and completely shattered the 5-meter-thick base of the neo-oak; the concussion pounded up through four floors of the house and wrenched at the three youngsters perched insecurely in the crown of the tree, surrounding them with a vast cloud of dust and deafening noise.

Then as the building itself fell outward in all directions, the gigantic neo-oak began to topple over . . .

Dust . . .

Dust from five stories of shattered cement was everywhere: Jonnath ran his fingers through his short cropped hair, and though his hand came away wet with blood, it was more grey than red. He tried to spit. Dust was jammed into his mouth, as if someone had stuffed it in deliberately. His head rang, and his right ear was deaf.

He tried to raise himself; his face had been half-buried in a pile of broken cement thick with the pulverized dust. Something was pinning him, holding him immobile.

A huge branch pressed down on his back, and he tried to push it away. A sudden jab of pain hit him in the left elbow, and he saw he had braced it on a piece of jagged metal that had cut his bare arm.

A vagrant memory of the night before flicked into his mind, but he brushed it away. Survival was first, right now. He moved his arm away from the jagged metal, and tried to flex his legs; nothing seemed to be broken.

He tried the branch again, and it shifted slightly—

enough for him to wriggle out sidewise. Aching in every muscle, he tried to stand, and after several attempts made it, leaning against another large broken branch, his head spinning as if he were spacesick, his mouth impossibly dry with the chalky taste of the dust.

The sun had just come up; the air was slightly damp, and quite chilly. A hiccupping whistle caught his attention, and he noticed an incongruous tickle bird, small and furry, that had recently been imported from Frenzle VII by his mother.

The thought of his mother made him cough several times, wrackingly; startled, the tickle bird flew away from the broken limb to a more distant one, and observed him curiously.

Where were the girls! Suddenly realizing, he looked about him wildly.

Sheira and Triez were nowhere to be seen.

He passed his hands over his face, and felt dizzy. *Internal injuries?* he wondered to himself. He called the girls' names, once, twice, and then felt another surge of dizziness. He sat down unsteadily on a slab—and heard a voice. It was weak, and calling for help.

Frantically he staggered to his feet and searched through the tangled pile of rubble that had been his home . . . there was the sonostove, a battered wreck, and then he saw the chair his father had been sitting on when the attack had come. Relentlessly he once more rejected memories of his parents as he continued to search for the girls.

His sense of time was warping, he realized; it seemed now as if he had been searching for the source of that faint cry for days, and it had only been minutes.

Then he found Sheira. She was stunned but alive, and seemed to have no major injuries, though a faint line down one cheek was slowly welling small drops of blood. Then she tried to stand, and it appeared that her ankle had been reinjured—perhaps broken.

As if in some nightmare come from spoiled food, Jonnath dimly was aware of Sheira's voice, asking if Triez were dead. He was sure she must be; all three of them could not have come safely through that terrible explosion. But he had too much to do before he could afford to listen to the grief within him.

Triez . . .

Somehow they fashioned a crutch for Sheira out of a stout branch. Minutes later, they found Triez, hanging in a tumble of branches, motionless.

Bitterness rose even higher in him. "Dead," he said harshly, spitting the word out as if it were more dust.

But Sheira pushed him aside fiercely, and somehow managed to scramble through the branches to the small body. She touched her sister's throat.

"Alive," she hissed urgently, "Help me get her down. There's a squad of Star Guards across the street. They may see me any minute!"

They struggled hurriedly with the limp form.

"I don't think they saw us," Jonnath whispered as they laid the girl on the ground. "Is she alive?"

"She was, a moment ago." Sheira placed her hand between her sister's small young breasts and waited a moment. "Her heart's still beating."

"She may have a concussion. I'll have to carry her."

"But . . . where will we go?"

Jonnath thought. "There's a possibility . . . if we can sneak through the gardens next door . . . there's a vacant mansion. We might be safe there."

He picked up the limp body and they started off, keeping as hidden from the street as they could.

It seemd months later to him that he was finally able to set down Triez. They were in a garden, hidden from flying sleds by a patch of ten-meter-high *ghlis*-plants with their giant leaves.

The younger girl had regained consciousness, and sat dazed as her sister tended her.

For a moment it seemed as if the blackness hidden inside his mind had blown away; they were safe for the moment, and all of them were alive. Presently he would catch his breath, and then he would start off.

They were in the garden of the silent home of Telvar Gri's brother Kilar Gri; Jonnath knew that he was off somewhere in the Zia Complex, and the Star Guards would not have visited here.

But Kilar reminded him once more of his father and mother. Suddenly he turned away from the two girls, and felt tears trying to force their way out.

He heard a movement behind him, and then Sheira placed her hand on his shoulder. It told him she understood, she would not hold it against him if he gave way, just this once, to the grief that surged within him. Sheira had cried already; Triez had not yet realized fully what had happened.

Then he was on his knees, choking and sobbing great dry racking heaves of grief that tore at him and stripped away his clumsy defenses.

Sheira kneeled behind him, stroking his back, saying nothing, as the paroxysms held him . . .

"It's awful quiet," whispered Triez a few minutes later, as they observed the silent home of Telvar Gri's brother.

It was supposed to be empty, of course; but the wide set of pictureplex insets that swept across the back of the whole first floor—the center one had been smashed.

Looters? Already?

Telling the girls to remain where they were, Jonnath moved carefully from cover to cover, approaching the broken segment of pictureplex.

Just inside the house, he discovered the body.

He was a poorly dressed Kalvaran, with a faded orange shirt that indicated he was a Controlled, a criminal who would never ordinarily have been permitted in this sector of town without a specific permit.

Jonnath searched the man's pockets.

No permit.

He was a looter, then. There must have been more than one; perhaps this one had gotten greedy and was disposed of by the others.

The others—who might still be inside!

It was a good thing he'd made the girls stay behind. Silently, swiftly, he searched his uncle's mansion.

He had been here many times before, and he could tell that looters had struck. The place was stripped of many lightweight compact valuables that were familiar to him, and things were in general disarray.

But apart from Jonnath, the place was empty once more.

He returned to the body with a huge sheet of sealing plastic, wrapped it, and dragged it into a closet. Then he went out into the garden and helped the girls inside.

He put Sheira on a sleepcouch and he and Triez dug out some tape for her ankle. Then Jonnath insisted Triez lie down too while he tried the multiwave tuner.

"—best thing about the multiwave," a tired voice said with a Kalvaran accent, as Jonnath reached a high band on the tuner. "They're virtually nondirectional. So *they* won't find me without some difficulty, and I'm not going to tell you where I am—or who I am. They seem to have a line on nearly all the important people on Kalvar; all I'll say is that they missed me somehow.

"I don't know who's listening, either, of course. But I'm hoping some of you have transmitters too, and can contact me. I'm going to try to act as a news center; you tell me what's going on where you are, I'll compile it, and send it out every half hour.

"One thing, though—*stay out of sight*. The Star Guards seem intent on three things, so far as I've found out: killing our leaders, evacuating the cities, and taking hundreds of thousands offworld for the Star Games.

"So don't get caught. Contact me at resonance 367. I'll be back on the multiwave in approvimately half an hour—if they haven't caught *me* by then. Good luck—good luck to us all." The strange voice broke.

Then transmission ceased.

"Evacuations," mused Jonnath. "That's why nobody was around except Star Guards and looters. They must have started from here—we've at the center of the city."

Sheira was asleep and Triez was weeping softly, nestled in Sheira's arms.

Jonnath went upstairs and took a sprayclean bath, then began searching Kilar's mansion more thoroughly.

There was food, plenty of it. Taking seconds to cook a small roast on the sonostove, he took it in to the girls, who were now both fast asleep on the couch. He cut off a portion for himself and left the rest for them when they awoke; they'd be starved, he knew.

Then he went to the library. The looters had not had time to solve the secret, but Jonnath knew it, and presently a bookcase section slid aside. In the small storage room this revealed, Jonnath found a small rack of pistols, rifles, and ammunition, both solid and explosive shells—neither kind would have any effect on the Star Guards, but if the looters came around again . . .

101

He loaded up on solid ammo, slung a Leeh rifle on his back, and stuck two Brun pistols in his belt.

Now they had food, arms, a reasonably safe place to hide. It was unlikely the Star Guards would check up on an abandoned mansion, especially since this section of the city had apparently already been evacuated.

The half-hour was up. He returned to the multiwave tuner and switched it on.

It hissed quietly; the unknown Kalvaran had not yet returned . . . or perhaps he would never return.

He looked up and saw Sheira regarding him silently, one hand protectively on her sleeping sister's head.

The multiwave tuner came to life.

"It's worse . . . much worse than I'd realized," came the voice of the unknown Kalvaran, sounding infinitely weary now.

"There is not a trace of Kalvaran military resistance left. The planet has fallen. The Star Guards are exterminating our entire leadership—everyone in government, the management levels of business, anyone with influence, power, money, reputation, they're being systematically slaughtered. They had most of us marked beforehand, that's obvious now.

"Did you know that every tenth planet, roughly, in the Zarmithan Empire has a Star Games arena of one sort or another? I didn't, but that's over seventy arenas. A hundred thousand lives a month." The man's voice broke.

"They're restocking from Kalvar. One of my informants has cracked the enemy's communications code; it seems their plan is to use about twenty-five percent of the population in the games over the next ten Standard months. After that they'll . . . slack off. Use us for a steady source. From then on.

"And there's nothing we can do about it."

It was beyond horror. Sheira looked at Jonnath, utter incomprehension on her face.

Jonnath's mind ran through the figures, and the man was right—there was nothing that could be done. The galaxy had a million inhabited planets in it—more than a million billion people—and no one would care what happened here. *For every million of us dead, a billion of them left,* he thought. *What do they care?*

102

No one would care.

"They don't want to occupy Kalvar," the tired voice said over the multiwave. "Its gravity is too strong. But they don't want us to be able to rise up against the garrison they'll station here.

"It's calculated terror. They want to bring down fear on the Ten Systems; the Zia Complex is about to fall apart, and they figure the Kalvar example will hasten Shaikon's collapse.

"They've got us three ways—we're to be an example, we're to help feed their bloody Star Games, and we're to be reduced to the status of an agricultural planet— every bit of industrial capacity we have is being destroyed or taken offworld.

"However, some plans have been suggested to—"

A sudden high-pitched screech came over the tuner, and a rough voice began speaking. *"Attention. Attention. This is the Chief Admiral of the Guards of Zarmith. Any inhabitant of Kalvar found listening to any unauthorized multiwave transmission will be shot. Kalvar is now a possession of Zarmith. We will brook no further interference with our plans. Authorized transmissions will be made only on resonance 171. A screamer circuit will be synched with the band you are now listening to. That is all.*

The high-pitched screech came back as the harsh, sardonic voice of the Chief Admiral cut off. Hastily Jonnath switched away from resonance 367.

He was tuning for the authorized resonance when he heard a distant shout.

Jonnath darted to the two girls on the sleepcouch. Triez had been awakened by the screamer circuit.

"Into the library, quick," said Jonnath. "I think I heard the looters in the garden. There's guns there—come on!"

They reached the library as the sound of more breaking pictureplex inserts arose. Jonnath left the door open slightly as he directed the girls to the hidden gun rack.

Peering out the door, he saw the looters entering through the newly shattered pictureplex—three of them, hard-looking men with orange shirts.

Each had rifles and pistols. Jonnath realized he was scared, terribly afraid. One of the men turned as he stepped through, and gestured at someone outside.

103

There was no more time for fear—he poked the muzzle of his Leeh rifle through the door, flicked the control to automatic, and sprayed the room they'd just left. His arm hurt with the recoil.

Two of the men dropped instantly; the third grunted with pain and fell to one knee, raising his Brun pistol and aiming it at Jonnath almost immediately.

The Leeh was empty; Jonnath ducked back into the library as four shots struck the heavy neo-oak door. Splinters flew as he reloaded with desperate speed, then paused to consider the situation.

There was a window opening onto the garden—anyone outside could come through it!

Another shot slammed into the neo-oak door, and Jonnath pushed it to and locked it, then dashed to the window. He ducked just as a shot came through it, starring the plastiglass.

He peered over the windowsill and saw one man outside, ducking behind a small tree. Jonnath set his rifle on the sill, switched to single fire, and took careful aim on the spot.

For a moment nothing happened; there seemed to be no other looters about except for the one still inside and the one behind the tree.

There was movement—the looter stepped out and sent a burst from his Leeh at Jonnath, firing high.

At the same moment Jonnath squeezed off two single shots. The man threw up his arms and toppled backward, lying motionless in the short grass.

Immediately Jonnath threw the window open and vaulted out into the garden, grunting with the pain in his arm. He raced for the inset of broken pictureplex, halted by it, and looked carefully around the jagged edge.

The wounded looter inside was detaching a small grenade from his belt—*a beta grenade?* thought Jonnath, with sudden fear.

No, he was pulling the pin; it was a conventional grenade—but he was going to blast down the library door. The girls would be killed!

Jonnath raised his rifle and squeezed the trigger. A shot rang out and the looter turned, startled, to face him. He had missed.

Now the looter was preparing to throw the grenade at

him—Jonnath flicked the Leeh to automatic and fired again.

A spray of solid bullets struck the looter in the chest and he windmilled backward, his arms waving, his legs kicking—then dropped the grenade.

Jonnath ducked as it went off with a thundering roar.

He peered back into the room after a moment; through the smoke he could see the shattered body of the looter, a torn red hulk toppled against the broken sleepcouch. Shuddering, he turned away.

The girls! He dashed to the library window and pulled himself over the sill, his arm protesting.

The girls were dazed; Triez was crying again, but this time Sheira ignored her, looking blankly at Jonnath as he entered.

"Are they . . . gone?" asked Sheira.

Jonnath shuddered again, involuntarily. He had *killed* them—he had killed four men. Men who hadn't really had a chance, men taken by surprise.

They would have killed him, of course. And the girls . . . they would have killed the girls, too—later.

"They . . . won't bother us," said Jonnath, unwilling to put into cold words what had happened. He sat down heavily and tried to think, while Triez cried and Sheira sat motionless.

He was never sure just how long he sat there, his nerves protesting the thousand indignities of the past day. But finally the neo-oak door caught his eye. It looked . . . strange. As if it had suddenly begun to char around the lock. His mind struggled to comprehend.

Then Triez screamed as the door crashed inward. A half dozen men in shimmering crimson burst in, past one in solid black holding the Nangee flasher he'd used on low power to burn through the door.

One of the men in crimson had a black helmet. It was he who spoke as the patrol stopped just inside the door.

"Well . . ." The man spoke with a kind of satisfied irony. "A noisy nest of Kalvaran, eh? How did you escape the evacuation? Ah, well, no matter. Shall I have you offworlded, or simply shot?"

The one all in black spoke up. "Captain Vaggar, they are only children; they'd go nicely in the Star Games, eh?"

"By Phanoc, that's so. Big for their age, Liathas; these

105

Kalvaran fool me all the time. The blonde one, though she's a beauty. Pity to waste that; the Lady Tza would be pleased with Krith Vaggar if I provided this one for her amusement. And the lad should struggle well in the games . . ."

Now Jonathan knew the taste of final defeat. Those crimson shields made them invulnerable. Kilar's rifles would be useless, except against the one in black, and the patrol had their pneumoguns out and ready. Not a chance.

Movement beside him—Triez. She was panicking; she'd had a pistol in her hand and had held onto it when the guards came in, and now she was raising it convulsively, aiming, blindly, firing—

"*No*," shouted Jonnath. "Triez—"

It was too late. Her pistol went off once, the bullet winking out harmlessly on the captain's shield—and one of the Guards fired his pneumogun. Its low 'phut-phut' was almost inaudible after the roar of the pistol—but Triez slumped to the floor, blood pouring from her head.

The captain swung toward the guard. "Borlat," he said harshly, "that was unnecessary. She couldn't have hurt—"

Jonnath went mad.

Guns couldn't get through the forcescreen—but perhaps bare hands could. After all, the guards weren't harmed by the field.

He leaped for the captain, hoping he could get his hands around the man's throat before one of the others could fire.

A second later he knew why they had not fired—as an inconceivable lance of pain wrenched through him the moment he touched the shimmering crimson field.

The shock from the patterned electricity convulsed his body. Screaming in agony, he slumped to the floor, half-senseless.

"Bressan, take the girl," he heard dimly through the waves of darkness battering at his stunned brain. "Borlat, you take the body; I want to have a double-check on all three identities.

"As for this one, he's brave but foolhardy. Liathas, a millior says he doesn't get through his first day as a gladiator . . ."

The pain faded away . . . he was passing out . . .
Captain Krith Vaggar . . . Liathas . . . Borlat . . . he
wouldn't forget . . . he'd come back from the Star Games
. . . avenge Triez . . . find Sheira . . . Lady Tza . . . Borlat
. . . Bressan . . . *Captain Krith Vaggar* . . .

3 The Arena of Death

THE ARENA STANK.

It stank of sweat and fear and blood and death.

It stank of stale sour wine and the effluvia of five
hundred years of human misery in the pits buried beneath it.

Jonnath sat naked beside an old man in a tattered loin
cloth, and knew that some time in the next few hours, he
was going to face death. His mind was clouded with
emotions and confusion, and he was desperately trying to
clear his mind of these irrelevancies, to learn all he could
before they called him forward to meet doom.

Survival—that was the only truth now. The past was
supremely irrelevant. Only training and knowledge could
help him now.

"Man and boy," said the old man, "I've seen 'em
come in and I've seen most of 'em go right back out,
for thirty years. Mostly because they're dom foolish."

Jonnath had been listening absorbedly to the old man
for the last fifteen minutes. For two days he's been im-
prisoned, with the rest of a shipment from Kalvaran, in
vast gloomy barracks elsewhere in the pit area. Then a
squad of men in brown had come through, selecting occasional individuals. Shortly thereafter, he'd found himself unceremoniously thrust into this anteroom, which was
nothing more than a large barred cage.

"Yep, I've figgered it out. Most of 'em, they're plain
scared. Freeze up, they do, moment they see what they're
up against. And—"

"But what *do* they come up against, Yissor?" Jonnath
looked about. There had been two rather clearly defined
groups in the cage when he had entered—twenty or so
nervous men and boys, none of them Kalvaran, almost

107

certainly newcomers to the arena as himself, and three or four others, including old Yissor, who had unconcernedly been sitting on the benches playing an idle game of Warp.

Yissor had dropped out of the game just then, so Jonnath had sat down beside him, slightly uncomfortable because of his nudity but determined to learn.

"Ah, now, lad," Yissor said in a kindly tone, "that's a long story, it is, and isn't much time till the numbers start coming in . . ."

Involuntarily Jonnath touched the spot at the back of his neck where they had burned in his number—LVC-100-15-195. Eleven letters and digits—and on the back of his neck where he couldn't possibly see it—but he knew he would never be able to forget it. The long line of prisoners, the guards with flashers, strong arms suddenly immobilizing him, then the stab of burning pain and the stench of his own flesh burning . . . he wouldn't forget that.

"Besides," Yissor continued, "he's got a powerful lot of different tricks to play, Pitmaster Sorvallian has. Stands to reason, y'know. They put these Games on here in Changar Arena three times a week Standard, after all. Mostly the same people watching every time, live and solido. Never seem to get tired of it, though if I'd ever Fought Free, I shouldn't have wanted to hear of the Star Games again myself. But lots of people watching lots of the time means they got to keep mixing it up, y'know."

Faintly, far off in the direction of the entrance to the arena floor itself, came the muffled sound of a series of screams, a sound of pounding on the great gate, more screams, silence. There was an animal roar.

Then the animal roar was drowned out by the roars of ten thousand people. Jonnath shuddered in spite of himself.

Yissor grinned. "Bear-wolf. Great crowd-pleaser! 'Course, there's a bunch of standard items; they use 'em about every time. While you was downstairs and the games started this morning, they let out about, oh, twenty-five of you tall fellers and your women into the arena, then sent a bunch of them winged things from that place where they make the poison, what is it, Karshon, yep. Only without the poison, of course.

108

"Their jaws were enough, I expect. Always are. I uster talk Pitmaster into letting me see the first part of the show, before I come on, but like I said, I got tired of it after a while."

"You mean . . . you've been here fighting for thirty years?" Belatedly Jonnath had realized what the old fellow Yissor had said earlier. In the arena—for twice Jonnath's lifetime! "How—how did you manage it?"

Yissor chuckled with amusement. "Most everybody makes professional the same way, 'cept for volunteers from outside—the real outside, that is, what most professionals don't talk about. Most of 'em pretend that out back there where we live, that's Outside. Pah." Yissor hawked and spat.

"But *how?*"

"Okee, you get sent out there the first time, the first few times out there, and you get through the assignments. If you look good, they let you start specializing after that; then they let you become a professional if the crowd maybe likes the way you do things. If they *really* like you, you get beat and they let you live. Well, I'm pretty good—there's a trick against them Karshon things, those flyin' slugs, I used about the third time out on my own. Let you in on it sometime, maybe. Anyway, after that I was in, so when I got caught by surprise oncet or twice later, they always let me get out of it."

"Is there any way for you to get out of the arena entirely? I mean, do they give you anything to hope for?"

"Usta be out all the time. Handsome, I was, and the rich ladies, they liked to have me around. Smelled of death, they said I did." He rubbed his hands along his thighs, and slapped his leg. "Then . . . well, they don't much bother to keep you young in the arenas, lad. After that I tried to Fight Free oncet, but halfways through I got a broke leg, and that stopped that."

Jonnath hated to appear ignorant, but he suppressed his instinctive reticence. "What is 'fighting free'?"

"Why, when they have the High Games, that's oncet a year, they allus offer a few of the top men the chance to fight their way out. Not too many takers, usually, seeing as how it means you fight twice a day for a week, taking on everything Pitmaster schedules for you. And dom few make it . . ."

Jonnath shook his head. "It's strange. I always thought once you were here, that was it. And if you were down, that was it."

"Aw," said Yissor, leaning back and rotating his shoulders to loosen the muscles, "the people out there—and don't ever forget to play to the solido cameras for the ones at home—they like their blood, but they like to see a good show, too. Otherwise, see, they wouldn't bother having professionals, and specialists, they'd just send everybody in to get chawed up."

The old fellow patted Jonnath on the shoulder. "And they got a lot of chawers to choose from, let me tell you. A lot o' planets have got a lot o' strange animals on 'em . . ." He seemed pleased at the thought.

Eagerly, Jonnath said, "You must know a lot of tricks about them."

"Oh, yeah," said Yissor. "You make it through this first week or two, I'll maybe let you in on some. Right now, though, it'd be out o' place for me to do that. Besides, you gotta make it on your own if you're gonna make it at all. Tricks is okee, but I wouldn't tell you none o' mine less I thought you could use 'em."

A terrible roaring sound echoed hollowly throughout the vast underground pit area.

Yissor drew Jonnath to the bars of the cage. "See him there, son? Look over there—" He pointed through the bars to a large ramp leading downward from the arena gate. "He's a mean 'un. From Zengg. A bear-wolf, they call 'em. Ain't he a beauty?"

The bear-wolf *was* beautiful in its own efficient, terrifying way. Jonnath estimated the beast was not quite as tall as he was, but was twice as broad in the chest and shoulders. A half-dozen snake ropes had been cast around his thick neck, their silvery sheen contrasting with his glossy black fur.

Huge seven-clawed paws battered and tore at the ropes which were pulling him away from his latest conquests out in the arena. Any of the pseudo-living ropes could hold a *bisfas*-beast; there were six of them simply because the men behind the ropes needed three on a side to keep the roaring bear wolf from getting away to one side or the other, and at that they were having a hard time of it with this one.

110

The bear-wolf's long, almost prehensile tail lashed about in fury. Jonnath admired the flowing brute power—until he saw the blood drying on the beast's jaws and claws.

He turned away—to meet the amused eyes of old Yissor.

"Heh, lad, you'll never make a professional if you can't stand the sight of a bear-wolf fresh from his kill!"

Jonnath was boyishly indignant. "My father trained me well in techniques of combat—human and alien. I could kill that animal with only a dagger."

Yissor grinned. "If you'd have been called out to face him today, son, you wouldn't even have had that!"

"Well . . ." said Jonnath, then shut up. Yissor was an old man; he knew much, much more about the arena and the Games. Jonnath could fight on his own for a year—for ten years—and not learn as much. "What animals will they send *us* out against?" he asked then.

Now Yissor laughed outright, his voice scaling higher and higher and breaking with an unpleasant cackle.

"The most dangerous animal of all, sonny; you walked right into that one!"

Jonnath looked puzzled. A commotion outside the caged anteroom almost drowned out Yissor's one word of explanation:

"Man!"

"Man?" said Jonnath, wonderingly. "What—"

The barred door of the anteroom swung open and a short, barrel-chested man with a large red beard entered, followed by three other men. All were dressed in brown.

"Pitmaster Sorvallian," whispered Yissor.

Pitmaster Sorvallian's voice cut through what little conversation had been going on.

"Okee, lads, up with it, lively. It's been a good show today, so they're looking for the best."

Yissor was on his feet again, flexing his stringy muscles. Jonnath marveled at how casually he was taking the call to go out in the arena. He knew he himself was frankly scared.

The Pitmaster spoke. "Waspo Dinnel, now's your chance to get promoted out of here. We've got a new batch of fresh ears, so we're filling up your ticket!"

Waspo Dinnel was one of the men Yissor had been

playing Warp with; he set down his markers and stood up, grinning.

"What's he so happy for?" Jonnath whispered to Yissor.

"Look how many fresh ears the pitboys are taking. That's why."

Jonnath watched uncomprehendingly; Sorvallian read off eight numbers and the three men in unadorned brown selected men from the batch that had been standing around silently and nervously. Jonnath realized now that all of these were naked, like himself.

"Has that one got to fight all of these? Is that it? But why is he so *happy* about it?" The naked men were all in good condition, while Waspo Dinnel was as short as the Pitmaster, and even had something of a fat belly.

"It's his specialty, sonny," Yissor said in a low tone. "Two longswords he gets."

"But what do they get?"

"Why, nothing!" Yissor sounded rather astonished that he should ask. "That's his specialty—he's got three minutes to kill all eight of 'em. Wouldn't do if they could *duel* with him, would it? Take too much time. Audience, they get bored seeing simple duels all the time. He'll get 'em, though. Been waiting for a year for enough to get assigned to him so he can make a proper impression. Wants to get transferred to a bigger arena, make some real money on bet tithes."

It was too much to absorb easily. Jonnath filed it in his mind, and tried to remember the seven ways an unarmed man could take a sword away from another man . . . could it be done at all when the other had two? He was glad he hadn't been picked for that.

The he thought he had an answer.

"Couldn't they gang up on him, though?"

"Now that's the first thing I told you, lad," Yissor said, testily. "They never will—they're too scared. Oh, maybe two of them will try it, or even three . . . but that's why Waspo's a specialist. They never make it past those two swords."

Then another of the professional gladiators was called by name, and two numbers were read aloud. Jonnath would have asked about that, but . . .

"Yissor," said the Pitmaster.

Jonnath tensed. Would they set him against someone who'd be too much for him? Old . . . he was so old . . .

"Nothing fancy today, I'm afraid, you tough old bis-fas." The Pitmaster slapped him on the shoulder. "Just the usual, but look out for him—he looks like he's fast on his feet for all his size!"

Jonnath frowned in puzzlement, then realized what the Pitmaster meant before he read off the number.

"You—LVC-100-15-195. Follow Yissor. You'll be on right after Waspo, Yissor, so make it good and keep the crowd happy."

The Pitmaster moved away. "Yissor, Yissor, am I going to have to fight *you*?" Jonnath felt sick inside. Why, he could kill the old fellow with one hand in two seconds!

They weren't guarding him, Jonnath saw as he stepped out behind Yissor onto one of the ramps to the arena. He could break and run.

But where to?

"Yep!" answered Yissor cheerfully. "About time they gave me someone that can step around lively out there. I get tired of the old ladies and cripples I usually draw."

"But—" Jonnath was appalled. "I'm no cripple, Yissor; don't you . . ."

Yissor was eyeing him gleefully. "Look, feller, you're just a fresh ear I pulled on the draw now. I like you but I like you better as an opponent. I don't *have* to tell you, but I'm gonna tell you what it's all about now."

A pair of sturdy armed men in brown stood at a counter at the head of the ramp. The roar of the crowd came louder now, through the arena gate only meters away.

Yissor slapped a thin hand on the surface of the counter. "Okee, lads, let's have 'er!"

One of the armed men disappeared through a barred gate that was half ajar, then returned with a tank that had a flexible hose attached to it. Yissor took the tank and the man helped him strap it onto his back.

Then he flicked a little switch. A thin, high-powered stream of liquid shot across the ramp. There was the smell of oil. "Primed and ready," Yissor said with satisfaction. "Come on, lad, we'll be on in a moment."

"What *is* it," asked Jonnath. "It doesn't look like a weapon to me."

"That's why you're fresh ears, sonny, and why I'll be

cutting yours off in a few minutes!" He cackled with laughter.

"Sonny, ain't you never seen a flamethrower before?"

Jonnath's scalp tingled, and he swallowed hard. "What . . . what do they give me to fight with?"

"Why, sonny, I thought I straightened you out on that. You don't get nothin' but the clothes you were born in."

Yissor flicked another switch, and a tiny flame appeared in the nozzle.

"See that?" he said, and flicked the first switch. A low thunderous *whoosh* sounded, and a pencil of flame sprang out at least ten meters long; then it cut off at the nozzle, making it seem as if something were following the bright flame, extinguishing it.

A strong smell of burned oil filled the area where they stood.

"See, sonny, you got one chance, they say." Yissor was fiddling with the nozzle now, as if adjusting some slight irregularity of the flamethrower's focus.

"I got me a tankful of fuel up here, see," and Yissor banged lightly on the tank with one bony knuckle; it did not ring, but gave off a dull *thuck*. "But I can't just stand out there, turn it on, and burn you down even if you run away. It cuts off, see, and it takes time before I can turn it on again. That's what makes the show. Gotta use some *skill,* I do; and skill is what I've got, sonny. That's why they like me here.

"Pitmaster knows the bigger arenas would love to haul me offworld, but Pitmaster, he won't let me go. We work well together, and I make all I want on bet tithes, so I'd just as soon stay here myself anyway. Well, sonny, it was nice knowing you! Here comes Waspo—listen to that crowd! I guess he made his time!"

But Jonnath paid little attention to the howling of the crowd, or to the figure of Waspo Dinnel as he came through the gate and passed them on his way to turn in his weapons.

He was thinking; thinking fast. Survival—a brief lifetime of his father's efforts to teach him survival—this would be the real test.

And to survive . . . he would have to kill an old man.

Would he be able to?

Would he have the chance?

114

4 Flames at Noon

THE FLOOR of the arena was covered with gleaming white sand. It was the first thing he noticed as they stepped out through the great gates, and it seemed anachronistic, curious in an age when mankind could create almost anything in synthetic material.

As he swiftly studied the arena, the tinted translucent dome, the ten thousand people in the half-filled seats, he realized the purpose of the sand.

Blood. During the fights it would provide sharp contrast. Afterwards new sand would be added to cover the old. The deaths of an hour ago would be forgotten in the expectation of more.

This time—*his* death?

An annunciator was booming out through the amphitheater, hushing the buzz of conversation among the multitudes.

As it spoke, Jonnath noticed a wavering, a colorless shimmering between the rim of the arena floor and the seats beyond. A force field—of course! In this ageless factory of gory death, the audience had no desire to become part of the spectacle . . .

"And now—Yissor! One of the most entertaining Specialists in the history of Changar Arena. Today he exercises his skills against a single youth picked from the ranks of our latest conquest, the planet Kalvar. Notice his unusual size. This promises to be an exciting display of artistic skill against strength and agility."

A desultory patter of applause coursed through the scanty audience. Yissor bowed low.

Quickly Jonnath tried to grasp the situation. The arena floor was roughly an oval. Its narrow width was perhaps one hundred meters, its longer perhaps one hundred twenty-five. The range of Yissor's flamethrower he judged from the one display Yissor had given him to be at least ten meters, and the flame stayed lit at least three to four seconds.

115

But there was one thing Yissor hadn't mentioned.

How quickly could he fire it again after it had gone out?

There was no time to think further. The annunciator was silent, the audience expectant. Yissor had straightened up and adjusted one of the straps on his flamethrower.

Suddenly the old man turned the nozzle in his direction and flicked the igniter.

A needle of flame lanced toward Jonnath. He dodged quickly to his right in a split-second—and slipped, falling heavily to the sand. But the flame had wavered to the left before he had moved. Apparently Yissor had guessed that he would go that way.

The flame winked out at the nozzle before Yissor could move it back toward Jonnath, and the lance of fire poured into extinction in the clean white sands of the arena. A small patch of oil burned slowly.

Jonnath felt his flesh creep a little with shocked realization—the flamethrower's range was at least twice what he had supposed.

The smell of burned oil filled his nostrils. He got to his feet and scrambled backward. He must get out of range of Yissor's next shot!

Five seconds ticked away before Yissor flicked the igniter again. Again the lance of flame spouted in a low arc toward Jonnath, now twenty-five meters from the old man.

Again he dodged to the right. But this time the old man had guessed correctly, the flame following him as if magnetized.

Jonnath put on an extra spurt of speed and outdistanced the flame again before it winked out.

He gathered his breath and rubbed his skinned knee. Again he moved backward and waited. Five seconds passed.

As Jonnath saw old Yissor flick on the igniter for the third time, he turned and ran straight away from him for ten meters, then turned—to see the flame almost on top of him!

Yissor was smoothly twisting the nozzle on the flamethrower to increase its range as Jonnath dived to the left desperately. This time the flame did not swerve. But it winked out nearby Jonnath, laying sprawled on the sand —forty meters from Yissor.

Jonnath was near one wall of the arena now; there was Yissor, still in the center of the oval, still able, it seemed, to reach him no matter how far away.

No, it couldn't be as simple as that, Jonnath thought. *must* be some limit to that thing's range!

Innate caution had kept him from rushing the old man immediately after his first shot; he didn't know how often the flame could be fired, and he didn't care to catch the full force of it in his chest in a suicide charge. There *must* be some limit to that thing's range!

There was only one way to find out. The five seconds were almost over as Jonnath made his decision and ran for the deep end of the oval arena.

A glance over his shoulder, and he saw the flame behind him, arching higher in the sky now and following him slightly to the lett.

He was almost to the deep wall of the arena when the flame winked out some ten meters short of him.

It had stayed on longer that time—but it had fallen short. So Yissor *had* deceived him about its duration. But it had only reached some fifty meters that time. Was that another deception?

No! Yissor had moved forward at last! The flame could not reach the entire distance from the center of the arena to the far wall!

And this time it was only four seconds till the flame lanced out. Jonnath now had his back to the far wall as Yissor trotted toward him, weaving the nozzle back and forth slightly. The flames poured into the sands not more than a body length away from him before going out.

Yissor would think he had no place to run now—and Yissor was approaching, a sardonic expression on his seamed face.

The flame soared; this time only three seconds had passed.

Jonnath watched the old man's hands carefully as the flame sped toward him. Then he dodged left as he saw the hands twitch right—but instantly the hands twitched left again, the flame lagging but following inevitably, inexorably.

Jonnath had only one real chance, of course. Close

117

with Yissor, wrest the flamethrower from him. Kill him.

So he continued running left, angling slightly toward the old man to get some distance between himself and the wall, dodging space.

It would be a dance of death. Time—how often Yissor could fire. Distance—how close Jonnath could get while the flamethrower was off.

Now the flame was off, and still Jonnath continued his angled run. He was only thirty meters away from Yissor, spiraling around him toward the center of the arena.

A two second pause only, and the flame shot out for five full seconds. Again Jonnath kept his eyes on Yissor's hands as the old man played the stream of fire like a water hose, following his evasive moves.

The flame was out. Twenty five meters to go.

He bluffed a run at Yissor. Two seconds and five meters later the flame shot out. Jonnath stopped short and dodged right, then left immediately.

Then Yissor's hands moved quickly in a complicated twist—and flames formed a ten meter wide lasso of fire around him!

The audience roared its approval at last.

The flame died. Jonnath was breathing heavily. But he had proved to himself the absolute limits of Yissor's weapon.

Dom, but it was hot! A sheen of sweat covered Jonnath's naked body. Which would run out first—his strength, or Yissor's fuel?

The dance of death continued under the blazing sun.

Once his foot slipped in a smear of burned-out oil, and he fell heavily to the sand. A last spurt of flame from Yissor struck his left arm.

The pain seared. Jonnath scrambled to his feet, ignoring the pain. The fine edge of his conditioning was wearing down. The fuel supply must have been planned beyond anyone's endurance. His strength could not last forever.

Attack was the only answer.

The next time the flame winked out, he dashed toward Yissor. It flashed on again after two seconds, weaving now in a complicated figure eight pattern. It was almost a solid sheet of flame.

Almost. Jonnath twisted among the wavering stream of fire, watching, watching the old hands twisting and turning the nozzle. Nearer and nearer to Yissor he ran, avoiding every loop and flick of flame.

Yissor's face showed worry, though the audience was applauding constantly now and shouting both their names. The flame cut off and Yissor moved backward. Jonnath was only fifteen meters away and moving rapidly toward him.

Two seconds, and the flame leaped forward again. Yissor whipped the flame back and forth desperately. But Jonnath evaded every maneuver, with what must have seemed a terrifying ease.

With the flame off once more, Jonnath was just too far to reach Yissor before the two seconds. He started for him, but not at full speed.

The two seconds ticked off—and just as the flame lit and began its mad plunge toward him, Jonath used all his Kalvaran strength, leaping a full two and a half meters in the air and forward.

Too surprised to move the nozzle, Yissor stood paralyzed as the youth hurtled toward him.

Jonnath struck the sand joltingly at Yissor's side, and knocked the nozzle from his numbed hands.

"Now," panted Jonnath, "now *you* suffer!"

He seized the wizened man and prepared to lift him high in the air.

"*No*," the oldster wheezed, "don't do it, you fool! You've won your life for today, but if you kill me they won't let you leave! Listen to them!"

The audience was applauding wildly now, cheering, and shouting "Yissor, Yissor," and "a Kalvaran!"

Jonnath was amazed. The crowd was fickle; it had wanted to see him burned alive, but was cheering him now—cheering both of them.

"But—" Jonnath was filled with rage. "But, you old filth, you would have *killed* me! Am I not to—"

"You think of me as a traitor, lad," said the old man, regaining some composure.

Jonnath now thought to step carefully on the flame-thrower's nozzle, and the old man grinned.

"It's my vocation, sonny, though not one I'd have chosen for myself back home on Aphry. You confuse *me* with my *job!*"

Jonnath's rage did not subside, though he let go of

Yissor. "You would have killed me—you would have killed me, with enjoyment. How can you pretend to—"

The annunciator boomed. "LVC-195-05-100 has defeated Yissor's flamethrower. The concensus is that both fought well and both shall live.

"The next event will be two novices against Yuitre Poqas of Ravallan and his sting dogs. This will be followed by . . ."

Yissor slapped Jonnath on the back. "Come on, lad, we must clear the field. They've got to clean up the mess before they can go on."

A large mobile hopper full of white sand had already entered the arena. Three men jumped out and began hurriedly covering up the many spots of oil, some of which were still burning dimly.

Jonnath's face was still flushed with anger as they neared the exit, but Yissor spoke calmingly.

"You're professional calibre, lad, you've proved that today. Now you're at the crossroads—are you going to *act* like a professional?"

Jonnath started to protest, but Yissor continued. "Or are you going to let your anger keep you down in the pits with the fresh ears?

"It's your choice, you know. Start off wrong and you'll never fight with a clear brain. You'll never live Outside with the gladiators.

"You'll die."

Jonnath shook his head in confusion. "What—what happens now?" he asked finally.

"Well, right now it depends on Pitmaster. He may send you out unarmed with the fresh ears a few more times, or if he feels you've already become a crowd pleaser, he'll likely give you some weapon next arena day and see how you work out. Likely that's what he'll do—you made a good fight out there, lad; I'm proud of you!"

"*Proud—of me!*" Jonnath shook his head. He couldn't speak any further.

They were on the giant ramps leading to the pits under the arena. Yissor slapped Jonnath on the shoulder once more.

"We part here for now, lad. It's Outside for me. Luck in the arena!"

They issued him a sword three days later, and "luck in the arena" suddenly became a familiar phrase. Like new found brothers the professionals crowded around him and Boslan Calsh, a dour man of thirty who was to be his opponent. It would be Boslan's second appearance in the arena also. The time before he had slain a Cailizard barehanded.

Yissor drew Jonnath out of the group.

"Don't be careless, lad—both of you are new to this, and we've no way of knowing *his* abilities." They looked toward Boslan. One of the professionals was acting out a favorite parry for him, illustrating his advice. Boslan stood impassive.

Yissor nodded toward the scene. "Don't forget—this time it's really to the death. *He* knows."

Still Boslan had said nothing . . . but underneath his blond shaggy eyebrows his eyes were following the professional's mime.

Jonnath turned away. "They'll want to see one of us slain out there today," he said. "I know that. We're both relatively unknown. The audience will want blood." He started to study the fact that this did not upset him. *Am I turning into a creature of the arena so quickly? Survival comes at a high price . . .*

Then the arena gates swung open. The crowd of professionals melted away as Pitmaster Sorvallian appeared. "All right, you've made your greetings, men. Back to the cage for selection. You two—Jonnath and Calsh—you're next."

"Luck in the arena!" the shout came back from the disappearing gladiators.

Jonnath and Boslan Calsh stood in the gateway to the white floor of the amphitheater. Presently the mobile hopper had finished its cleanup operation.

"Who won?" asked Jonnath of the Pitmaster. "I didn't see anyone come off."

Pitmaster Sorvallian grinned hugely. "No one won, fellow! Best show in months! A dozen men in a fightout with Pwel multiswords, last man alive to win. Ha! Every dom one dead—the audience went wild! So you've got a tough one to follow . . ."

The hopper whined past them and they could hear the annunciator. Sorvallian turned to follow the hopper.

"Luck in the arena," he said over his shoulder, and was gone. Jonnath and Boslan Calsh looked at each other.

"Er, luck in the arena," Jonnath said hesitantly.

Boslan smiled, grimly. "Luck in the arena . . . but I'll trust to skill." His face returned to impassivity.

It was even hotter on the white sand than it had been the first time. Sweat covered Jonnath's body even before the annunciator was finished. The audience seemed to be paying little attention, still buzzing over the last event.

Then it was time to fight. Boslan Calsh went into a crouch and moved toward Jonnath.

Jonnath now smiled grimly. Already he saw that, although Boslan carried his sword well, he let the point droop too low.

Boslan attacked swiftly and Jonnath parried the older man with ease, his hilt low and forcing the other's point away. But Boslan was swift, and darted sideways, suffering only a shallow gash on his left arm.

It was hot work. The crowd was not paying much attention yet. The thought irritated Jonnath.

Boslan was a good fighter, but uninspired. Jonnath realized after several more swift engagements that he could take him when he wanted to.

But then what would he do?

Could he kill this man, as Yissor had said the crowd would insist upon?

Certainly Boslan would kill him if he were able, and he *was* a good fighter.

Another engagement . . . two . . . three . . . four . . . the heat made sweat run down their bodies. They engaged once more—and Boslan's sword flew through the air at least ten meters.

The crowd seemed to catch its breath as one being, and suddenly all eyes were now watching, waiting, expectant, as Boslan stood unarmed and Jonnath paused, bewildered.

The annunciator came alive. Yissor had told him of the electronic talley made of the audience's verdict. Each seat had a device to indicate his voice, and the solido-viewers at home had a similar device.

Doom was swift, in the arenas of death.

"The consensus," said the annunciator, "is virtually

122

unanimous. LVC Jonnath will slay MRX Boslan but may not claim right of properties."

Right of properties? Yissor hadn't mentioned that—but there was no time to wonder; he had to decide what he was going to do. He *couldn't* kill an unarmed man!

Boslan Calsh broke under the pressure.

With an animal sound of fear he turned and ran for the closed gates of the arena, a few meters distant, and banged on them hysterically.

Slowly Jonnath approached him . . .

. . . and then he knew what to do.

He threw his sword away and called to the desperate Boslan.

Boslan turned; his eyes widened when he saw Jonnath was now unarmed, and he launched himself immediately at the waiting youth.

It didn't take long. Jonnath's strength was too great for any ordinary non-Kalvaran. There were a few moments of struggle—then a soggy *snap*. Boslan's limp body fell to the floor of the arena.

There was a loud round of applause, mixed with wild shouts of approval. After a brief pause, the annunciator spoke again.

"Consensus is now that LVC Jonnath be granted fifty percent right to the property of MRX Boslan. There will be a half hour pause to prepare for the afternoon's special entertainment, which will symbolize the destruction of the Kizelay-Jalali Grand Fleet last week by our forces operating from Kinkaid's Star World . . ."

Jonnath retrieved his sword and strode to the exit. There was another spatter of applause; he stopped, turned, and raised his sword in the air in recognition of their approval.

"An inspired touch!" said Yissor. They sat at a rough wood bench by a large round table, in a large open air courtyard. Alien star patterns twinkled above them as they drank mugs of strong Lashkari ale in the chill night air.

"Inspired—to throw away your sword and kill him with your bare hands!" This was another gladiator, a sturdy man with only one eye. Jonnath basked in the unaccustomed praise and savored the taste of the ale.

Yissor's eyes gleamed shrewdly. "A bit squeamish about cold-blooded killing, weren't you, eh?"

"I—I couldn't do it, Yissor," He had to be honest, he felt; *something* decent had to remain. "Not that way. I guess I'll never be a real professional—not that I really want to be, either."

"Ahhh," grinned Yissor, "but you haven't the choice of it, you know. You're Outside here, with the rest of us, you've pocketed half of Boslan's miserable possessions, you've got all the skills. Why, with gimmicks like that, you may end up one day in Yarmith Grand Arena itself, or Tansavar, or Kinkaid's Star World!"

"Survival comes first, I suppose," said Jonnath quietly. "A few coins from a Boslan hardly make it seem a better life, though. The price of survival is high . . . almost too high."

But as Yissor had said, he had all the skills. As a professional gladiator, he now had to fight only once a week, usually. During the rest of the time he was allowed to practice with the vast store of special weapons from countless planets.

Telvar Gri had trained his son well in many forms of combat and with many weapons—but there were far more available in the arenas of the Star Guards.

Jonnath learned of the sting sword of Amalgarth, which caused an agonizing burning sensation when it opened a cut. He learned of the bolo knife from Dance, of the Luyhold cat spear, the Ihabab armygun, the Webb flying mat, the Pwel multisword, the Ratatosk firelight.

Each of these, and many others, was a separate study, requiring days, weeks, even months and years to gain a proper mastery.

Some of them Jonnath never learned; there was never time for everything. Others, Yissor tutored him in, until he became as widely skilled, in Yissor's opinion, as ninety-five percent of the professional gladiators in the whole arena system.

The thing that in the long run perhaps surprised Jonnath more than anything else was that it was a *dull* life.

For three years he fought once a week in Changar Arena, men, animals, even ambient plant forms from the

Magellenics, depending on the supply of each and the whims and artistry of the Pitmaster.

His specialty was not to specialize, and he became as much a favorite in his own way as Yissor in his. It delighted the crowds that, except when his opponent was sufficiently skillful for him to be forced to kill him in the fight itself, Jonnath would disarm him and, if the verdict was for death, as most of them were, he would throw away his own weapon and kill the man with his bare hands.

Thus it was that he became quite a popular figure, and the crowds began granting him more and more percentages of his opponents' wealth. He acquired a small amount of money that enabled him to live as comfortably as a gladiator could . . .

But he was feared as a fighter sufficiently that he was never permitted beyond the arena or through the gates of Outside, though others were.

It was a dull life.

In the third year of his captivity, at the age of eighteen, Jonnath was transferred from Changar Arena, over many protests.

It wasn't freedom. But it was a step forward.

5 Swords of Vengeance

JONNATH sat on the ground in front of his tiny new one-room hut in the Outside, observing the chill of late evening and the alien pattern of stars overhead in the night sky of Tansavar.

The sounds of carousing still drifted through the darkness. Jonnath had not joined them this first evening, but he knew what was happening. Professional gladiators were allowed many of the privileges of free citizens. Thus the Outside—once more he smiled bitterly at the inherent self-deception in the gladiators' term for what was still a prison—was in many ways like any ordinary small village.

There was wine and ale, and the stronger brews and liquors, and drugs, both benign and malignant; all that man in his half a dozen millenia among the myriad stars of the galaxy had discovered or devised.

There was food, choice food, and an atmosphere of rough camaraderie—and there were women, for women were ever attracted to rough men with money.

Most gladiators had money, there was no doubt about that. There was constant wagering on the progress of events in the arena, and it was an old custom to give a certain percentage of one's winnings to the professional who had won against strong odds. Inevitably the money became spread around, with the gladiators' own endless bouts of gambling and wenching and drinking—though seldom enough of that to impair their fighting skills, on which their lives depended.

Jonnath became aware of a tall figure approaching him with a sputtering torch of Djelgarth pine held high and away from his body. The wind was blowing down the narrow path between the huts toward Jonnath, and he could smell the characteristic and oddly invigorating special aroma of the Djelgarth pine mutation.

"Ho, Kalvaran!"

Jonnath came to his feet instinctively as the greeting came. Then he saw that the newcomer was fully as tall as he himself was—if not a few inches taller.

"What—who are you?" said Jonnath, puzzled.

"Willan Vis of Kalvar, hutbrother."

"Hutbrother?"

"Didn't that fool of a pitman tell you? I live here— and we have a standing bribe in to the pitmen for new Kalvaran to be assigned to us."

"*Us?*"

The newcomer reached the hut and vigorously drove the base of the torch into the soft earth in front of it. Then he drew himself up to his full height and studied Jonnath.

"By Phanoc if you don't look familiar!"

Jonnath gave his name, then said, "Willan Vis—that sounds familiar to me. Are you from Kallor?"

Willan smiled broadly. "No, Jornagar; but I remember you now—you're Telvar Gri's son. We met five years ago. You were . . . what, twelve? No, you must have been older, from the size of you now! And I was fifteen. It was at the Survival Camps—a dying tradition then, and

126

now . . . who knows?" A cloud passed over the taller man's face.

Then Jonnath remembered. "Willan! By the—yes! You beat me in the High Climb. I've never forgiven you that!"

Willan's grin matched his own.

"Yes, and do you think I was happy to have a bisfas calf of twelve edge me out in the Three Weapons class?" Willan chuckled and grasped Jonnath's shoulders.

"It's late now, but tomorrow evening after you fight, come along with me and meet the rest of us! I knew we could expect a good man if he'd been transferred up out of Changar Arena. They've a nasty habit of holding on to everyone they've got that's halfway competent. It takes a real stand-out to catch the attention of the bigger arenas sufficiently to make them take the trouble to pry him away from Changar, let me tell you. Ah, well, it's time for sleep. Many tomorrows to talk . . ."

"Are you the official reception committee?"

Willan laughed. "Much more than than, Jonnath Gri, much more than that!"

Tansavar had been one of the first planets captured by Zarmith II three hundred years before, when it began its march of conquest. And Tansavar Arena was now one of the three greatest in the Zarmithan Empire, surpassed only by that on Zarmith itself and the one on Kinkaid's Star World.

Tansavar Arena was vast almost beyond comprehension to Jonnath, who had become used to the modest Changar Arena—Tansavar held its games in a huge stadium capable of holding a quarter of a million spectators, and its huge pit complex underneath held at least ten thousand fresh ears—thirty thousand for brief periods during the bigger shows. The contingent of professional gladiators was some ten thousand strong.

The floor of the arena was a square at least two hundred meters on a side, with a smaller area marked off in it for limited contests. Each seat in the audience had a small solido viewer for close-up enjoyment of these latter.

As he stood in the small center area, Jonnath realized that for the first time in over two years, he was nervous. *Will I be good enough here?* He had become the best fighter in Changar by the time he had left. *But if they send me out against the best in Tansavar . . .?*

He was doubly nervous, as they had sent him in unarmed as if he were a fresh ears, and naked except for a rough cloth breechclout. He would have been indignant, but he knew they meant he would have to earn his dignity all over again here.

A man emerged into the center area, and Jonnath squinted against the sunlight, tinted blue by the translucent dome.

The man was armed! A small rawhide shield in his left hand—*that's silly,* Jonnath thought, *I'm unarmed*—and an Amalgarthan sting sword in the other, a meter long serrated blade that Jonnath had tasted just once before and wanted no more to do with.

The annunciator boomed. "A professional from Kalvar, unarmed because of his great size, LVC Jonnath. Against Zelavan Gannit, formerly a corporal in the Star Guards and now condemned as a thief. He is armed with Amalgarthan weapons. Nobilities, an interesting match of speed and strength against arms and skill. I invite your most careful attention . . ."

Jonnath noted the transparent forcefield barrier, some twelve meters high, that walled off the twenty meter square he and the other were now to fight in. *Not much space to maneuver in,* he thought.

The ex-Star Guard began moving toward him, waving the tip of the slender sting sword in a menacing arc.

Then Jonnath recognized him.

One of the members of the patrol that had kidnaped Sheira—and had shot down Triez!

Zelavan Gannit paused involuntarily at the look of sheer hatred that flashed onto Jonnath's face then.

I'd almost forgotten, Jonnath thought. *And they put one of them into my hands!*

Choking down a surge of blind rage, and ignoring the threat of the sting sword for the moment, he ripped off his rough cloth breechclout and stood naked in the center of the arena, wrapping the cloth around his right forearm. Almost suffocated with the need for vengeance—at last! —against one of the men who had wrecked his life, he still realized that he would have to rely on his brains.

128

Survival—survival first, and the only strategy open to an unarmed man: evasion.

A lifetime of training took over, suppressing the ache for vengeance into a dull throbbing.

Zelavan Gannit had recovered from his moment of startled amazement and was advancing carefully toward him.

The man was a thief, thought Jonnath, *but he had been a Star Guard. That means he knows how to fight.*

It was hot and dusty work. It was constant vigilance, avoiding the thrusts of the Star Guard, trusting his younger body, strong from his three years of constant fighting, would outlast the older man.

It was sweating and slipping in the sand and always, always, keeping out of reach of the sting sword.

After five minutes it was clear Zelavan Gannit was tiring, Jonnath thought, with a sudden hungry urge to have it over with. The fifty thousand in the audience were becoming interested in the struggle; he could sense their growing attention. There were hardly any crowd noises now except for a cheer at a particularly spectacular evasion on his part. *They're with me!* he thought, and the professional in him was pleased.

When it came to a climax, it was over in a flash.

Jonnath darted suddenly forward; Zelavan's tired sword arm could not swing the blade with full force, and the garment on Jonnath's forearm stopped its impact almost completely.

Almost—and Jonnath went mad. His right arm felt as if it were bathed in one of the old Yissor's flamethrower bolts as he closed with the Star Guard.

Zelavan attempted to swing his rawhide shield, to catch Jonnath at the key point under the ear—but Jonnath's arms were on him now, tightening, tightening . . .

The dead body of Zelavan Gannit slumped to the sand. Jonnath stood over him, staring down at the motionless figure as the killing rage slowly ebbed away.

Vengeance? thought Jonnath. *Is this what it is?*

He shuddered, and did not even hear the waves of applause as they rolled down from the tiers of seats and echoed across the floor of the amphitheater.

There was no elation in him. He felt only tired, and vaguely disgusted with himself.

Jonnath felt ill at ease. Willan strode along in front of him, holding a sputtering torch to illuminate the evening gloom.

He thought about his vague unease; it would be non-survival to ignore any warning, even as tentative as this was.

They were nearing a large open space filled with light and smoke and noise and laughter and the smell of drugs and alcohol when he realized what was troubling him.

He was not the only Kalvaran here! In fact, as he entered the wide courtyard he became aware of hundreds of his quasirace boistering loudly among other, smaller men.

He grinned wryly to himself; he was jealous! No longer was he to be the largest, most teared man in the arena; now he was only another Kalvaran—and far from the largest, as a quick scan of the crowd told him.

I hadn't realized I'd become vainglorious, the rueful thought came.

"There's something you don't see in most arenas," Willan said. "Over there, with Pitmaster Ishau. He's unique himself, for that matter—he treats us as fair as he can in his job, and the money we slip him keeps him convinced we are . . ."

Jonnath thought to defend Sorvallian, but shrugged and let Willan talk.

"But I meant the girl, the one he's got his arm around —Tarshia. As you can see, she's a Blue—from Abbess, you know. And . . . she's a professional gladiator! There's hundreds like her here. It makes life a lot more interesting . . ."

Jonnath was amused at Willan's talkativeness, as he observed Ishau; whose hands were with an odd gentleness caressing the delicate blue shoulders of a lovely Blue from Abbess. Judging by how pale the typical blue tint had become, she had left—or been taken from—Abbess at least ten years ago.

"Female specialists? Interesting."

"Oh, yes, interesting," Willan answered as he looked about the gathering. "She duels with Alsk pin guns. Very popular. Hasn't lost since—"

Willan broke off and signaled to a group of Kalvaran who had been studying the acrobatic dancing of a trio of young girls, none of whom could have been over fourteen years old Standard.

"You'll notice," said Willan, returning to the subject of Tarshia briefly, "that small bulge at her waist? Yes. That's Pitmaster's humor. She carries her weapons—he lets 'em all do that. It lets them carry on courtships on their own terms . . ."

Jonnath grinned, as the half dozen Kalvaran approached them and greeted Willan heartily.

"This the one from Changar, eh, Willan?" The speaker was more than a head taller than Jonnath, physically a giant of a man even for his planet. His eyes were slanted in what was called the oriental fashion, though no one really knew why. To Jonnath it simply meant that he came from the southeastern part of Central Continent, on Kalvar.

Willan introduced him as Adalph Ril. "Just about the best professional gladiator in the business, too, Jonnath."

The huge Adalph frowned slightly. "Alerting 'em again, eh, Willan?" He extended his hand palm up and placed it on Jonnath's shoulder in welcome.

Jonnath returned the gesture; then the large paw was removed from his shoulder.

"Defend or die!" Adalph shouted the ritual warning suddenly, and drove his two hands forward, the stiffened fingers aimed directly at Jonnath's solar plexus.

The blow would have meant death had it landed; and even Jonnath's arena-honed reactions would have been hopelessly slow had it not been for the instant of warning.

There was no time for thought; it was instinct that brought his own hands up to grab Adalph's, at the same time that he threw himself backward.

Adalph pitched forward and past him, landing heavily a meter away. Jonnath recovered his footing and stood warily over the large figure as Adalph lay on the ground, shaking his head to clear it.

"Is this guestly?" Jonnath asked heatedly, angered at the unprovoked attack. "Or did I somehow offend—"

Adalph turned onto his side, then sat up on the ground slowly. He shook his head once more, then grinned up at Jonnath. "Old arena joke: I almost kill you . . ."

Willan helped the giant up. "You might call it hazing," Adalph said, ruefully. "I like to knock a bit of the cockiness out of the new men after their first victory in Tansavar Arena."

"Dom unfriendly," muttered Jonnath, then grinned in spite of himself. "You should have told me; I can play to a script!"

"Ah, well," said Adalph, brushing himself off and looking around at the other Kalvaran. Their faces remained serious and impassive. "Let's get off to ourselves with these friends of mine here, and perhaps we'll tell you some things that will . . . interest you."

"Willan, is this straightness? Or more tricks?"

"No tricks, Jonnath. Come along and hear us out."

So he did. Now eight Kalvaran sat inside a large hut, while a tumble of neo-oak branches blazed merrily. The thin harsh smoke spiraled upward swiftly through an opening in the roof.

"There are over ten thousand professionals here in Tansavar Arena, lad," Adalph was saying.

Jonnath sipped from his bowl; the drink was an excellent imitation of Kalvaran qaat, strong, tart, and warming. The introductions had taken much time, and, to Jonnath's surprise, there was an unusual emphasis on the old style guestly rituals.

"All but about a thousand of these professionals are our countrymen of Kalvar."

Now that was mildly interesting; he began concentrating more closely on Adalph's words.

"There are several reasons for this. What started it all, of course, was simply that with the enslavement of Kalvar, the death arenas of Zarmith were glutted with hundreds of thousands of us." Adalph spoke with a careful, emotionless precision. Jonnath realized it was the only way the matter could be sensibly discussed, uncluttered by the bitterness and rage and sorrow of the last three years.

"Many of us were, of course, killed very quickly. Even for us of Kalvar it is difficult to stand up unarmed against the more exotic and dangerous galactic denizens. The Star Guards pluck well for their shows. Nor is it easy even for Kalvaran in a group to stand up under pin guns, flamethrowers, sting swords, hopthrows, snow darts, in the hands of specialists.

"In three years at least four million of us have been slaughtered in the arenas.

132

"But many of us did *not* die—as, for instance, you did not die. Not all of us were sent out to sure death."

Jonnath had grown restive; he broke in. "Naked against a flamethrower, they sent me first. No death is *certain.*"

"Mmmm," said Adalph noncommittally. "They sent me out first against a Zengg bear wolf. They were thoughtful about it, though; they broke my right arm beforehand . . ."

Jonnath blinked. No one else changed expression; there was no way for him to tell whether he was being jibed at. He let it pass.

"Now then," Adalph continued calmly, "with the natural Kalvaran advantages it is not surprising that quite a number of us did survive, quite out of proportion with the usual survival rate of Zarmithan captives. Then, as proven excellent fighters, we became sought after by the larger arenas—I am given to understand that we are now in the majority in all of the nine largest—and as Kalvaran, we also tended to have a great deal more comradeliness, more of a sense of common purpose.

"Common purpose—that is the crux! Originally, our only plan was to band together, to get as many Kalvaran in one spot as we could. This we did; as top fighters we acquired considerable money, and pooled much of it for careful bribes."

Jonnath saw an objection. "But didn't the Zarmithans suspect that something was up when so many of you began grouping in one arena?"

Adalph spoke sharply. "Not at all. You forget what we are in the arenas for—to fight. And . . . kill. Kalvaran are better fighters. They like to see us work.

"And they like to see us die; sixteen thousand of us have, here in Tansavar the last three years.

"Good fighters are good killers, Jonnath."

A dull anger began to grow in Jonnath. "But you *do* nothing. They make you kill each other and you do nothing at all. With such skill many of you could Fight Free in the High Games. That's what I plan to do."

Adalph shook his head. "No answer, that. Perhaps a hundred might Fight Free in a year—throughout all the arenas. You know it's unheard of for more than two at a time to fight free from any one arena. What kind of a solution is that? No, Jonnath, by our natural superiority

133

we are coming into a majority in more and more arenas—and now we have a chance for all of us to fight free. But in a way which . . . will not please our masters."

"Bah," said Jonnath, "you mouth words. You cannot rebel against the Star Guards, in spite of your numbers here. Their forces on Tansavar alone must outnumber you by twenty to one—not to mention their forcefields and weapons."

To his surprise, the other nodded agreement; Willan broke in. "You are right, of course—if it were only a matter of *our* weapons against theirs. But that's the point, because—"

"Enough, Willan," said Adalph, his face now stern. "Perhaps we have made a mistake in judgment with this young fellow. He seems only to desire his personal freedom—"

"Not my freedom—my revenge! My parents, murdered. The girl I was to marry carried off, her sister slain in front of us. No, Adalph, Willan, I fight free when the High Games come—and then, revenge!"

Adalph rose to his feet slowly, unsteady with anger that shook him. "*You* want revenge. *You* want freedom. Did you ever hear of a planet named Kalvar, gladiator? Did you know its cities were destroyed, a tenth of its population slaughtered, its people reduced to barbarism or carried off to die hideous deaths beneath alien suns? Revenge! Why, your loss is as that of a child's rattle when the house was burned to the ground." Adalph's voice trembled with rage.

Slowly, calmly, Jonnath stood. "Sir, my father, Telvar Gri, was one of the Grand Councilmen of Kalvar. What he taught me I have not forgotten. We saw the Tower of the Grand Council blasted to dust—with many of my father's friends inside it, men I have known since my childhood. I saw the empty city of Kallor. I heard a voice on a hidden multiwave transmitter tell of the rape of Kalvar.

"I have not forgotten, Adalph. But I have not forgotten my parents, beamed down almost in front of my eyes. I have not forgotten the girl that was to have been promised to me that night, nor her father, slain with my parents, nor her sister—twelve years old and slaughtered in front of me as if she were not a human being but a rat or a jord.

"I have not forgotten three years of fighting against all the hellish nightmares of Changar Arena.

"And since I fought alone for three years, I shall fight alone now, and when the High Games come, by Phanoc I'll cut my way free with my own sword and my own skill. I shall track down every single man on those two patrols, and—"

Adalph gestured impatiently. "Very well. You are not the first to have chosen his own way. If you change your mind, we may then tell you of *our* plans for the High Games."

"So be it." Jonnath smiled with grim pride, then strode out the canvas door.

Only a few men and women were left in the courtyard. Automatically he looked up at the stars to judge the time of night, then cursed when he saw the unfamiliar orientation of the constellations. Tansavar and Changar were far closer to each other than either was to Kalvar, and he recognized many familiar stars. But the planetary axii were, of course, different; and he could not even guess, with the distortion, what hour of the night it was. "Dom," he muttered to himself, "I don't even know what Tansavar's period of rotation is."

From the shadows surrounding the large hut, a larger shadow detached itself. Jonnath started involuntarily, then chuckled at his fear.

It was only a bisfas beast. This one gave a typically half-human cry, and extended one triangular ear to be scratched.

He scratched the lumbering friendly animal, then started to walk away, toward his hut. "Let Willan come when he wishes," he said aloud.

As he walked, he became aware that the bisfas was following him. He smiled in the darkness. "Lonely, eh?" he said, and scratched the extended ear again. The bisfas grunted with contentment, and continued to walk with him.

"Ah, well, after tonight I suppose I'll be lonely again myself." Jonnath shrugged. "Perhaps I shouldn't have spoken out against them as I did."

135

The bisfas moved closer to him, rubbing his shoulder against Jonnath's.

"Hey, you're a huge one," said Jonnath. "Over five hundred kilos, I'd guess. As tall as I am!"

The bisfas cocked his head at him and blinked.

"I could swear you were grinning at me, you old . . . How can anything with a face as sad-looking as yours possibly grin?"

Now they were at the hut. Jonnath started to enter; then he spun about and hunkered down in front of the door. The bisfas beast loomed over him.

"Gotta think this out," said Jonnath, still talking aloud. "Listen to this, fella," he continued, addressing the bisfas as if he were an old friend. "I meet one of the men I'm looking for— meet him in the arena. What do I do? I kill him. Sounds logical, maybe. Maybe it is.

"Then I'm approached by some Kalvaran. They offer to let me in on their secret plot to . . . I don't know, take over the planet, I suppose. They seemed pretty confident, even if it's obvious they wouldn't have a chance of succeeding at a revolution.

"But I suppose I should have listened to them. And I suppose I shouldn't have killed Gannit, at least until I'd gotten some information out of him—where the others have gotten to in the last three years, maybe even where they took Sheira.

"So that's two stupid things I've done today. I don't suppose there's much I can do about it now. But it would be nice if I could remember to stop and think before I act. If I'm quick with my body and mind in the arena, that's fine—for the arena. Time I started using my mind Outside."

He looked up at the distorted constellations—the old ones that were much the same here as on Kalvar: the Wheel, the Flame of Irridar, the Ship, the Bones, the Seven Jewels of Korkasshoth, Miliagre, the NQP—and the new ones he'd learned on Changar: the Tiny Bells, Gilgamesh's Pipe, the Brandy Tree, and that strange one that bore no resemblance to its name, the Archer. He remembered old Yissor telling him once that Changar people thought it had to do with a certain folk hero from shortly after the discovery of the multiwave, but that actually it went back to the original Earth constellations.

136

Old Yissor, an odd one. An aged student of death who knew astronomy . . .

Jonnath yawned, got to his feet, scratched the shaggy triangular ear of the bisfas once more.

"Dom foolish I am," he said, "standing here talking to a bisfas when I should be getting to sleep. I wonder what's been the stupidest thing I've done today . . ."

"I'd say it was killimg that Star Guard im the arema, Jommath," said the bisfas beast, and wiggled his ears for another scratch.

6 Master of the Star Games

"RIGHT," said Jonnath.

Then he stepped back, stunned, and looked at the bisfas.

There was a pause.

He looked at the bisfas uneasily; the bisfas seemed to return the uncertainty.

The pause continued.

"Okee, Willan," Jonnath said at last, "where are you? It's a good trick, but what's the point of it?"

He paused again, expecting Willan or some practical joker among the camp of professionals to step out from behind the hut.

Then he blinked.

The bisfas was slowly shaking its head.

"Mo," said the bisfas, his voice lower and more rasping than a human being's. It seemed oddly *thicker,* too, although the only sound that seemed intermittently to suffer was the "n."

"Mo, Willam is still at the meetimg hall, Jommath. It is I, M'romgovorth, Cheltam-brother of Obas Limm. I speak for myself amd you are the secomd humam I have spokem to."

Now Jonnath shook his head, first slowly and then more determinedly, as he walked backward until his foot hit the wall of his hut.

"No, it's a joke, a trick, I can tell that. You might as

137

well give up, whoever you are. I'm in no mood to play games tonight with tricksters."

"Okay, Jommath, I will prove I am what I say."

"What's 'okay'?"

"Sorry; archaicism; you would say 'okee.' "

"Mmm. That's supposed to convince me? Or is the fact that your lips are moving supposed to do it? I can think of three ways that could be managed with the proper electronic equipment, and—wait a minute."

Jonnath ran his hand around the bisfas beast's neck, searching for a voder dot, leads, implantations.

There was nothing.

"Feel my throat," said the bisfas.

Jonnath groped through the shaggy fur below the animal's jaw, and touched the warm skin. Then the bisfas continued to talk to him.

And Jonnath felt vocal cords vibrating precisely with the words.

"You see, it is mo trick, Jommath."

"What . . . what are you?"

"A mutamt. I am mot sure of the mathematics that apply, but I have estimated that a mutatiom of this order of magmitude occurs mo oftemer tham omce every five humdred years."

"Then there have been others like you?" He wondered at his own lack of astonishment—but that would come later, he supposed.

"I do mot mo, but I suspect it. Umfortumately, the others must mot have beem as lucky as I was." M'rongovorth gave a low growl, which sounded to Jonnath as if it were meant for a sigh.

"Lucky, because evem for homo sapiems I would be comsidered a gemius, but a gemius living among idiots would grow up am idiot. Amd my kimd are mot evem as imtelligemt as idiots. Mo, I had to have a teacher—amd I was lucky emough to have ome, though he did mot mow it umtil the emd."

Jonnath shook his head as if to clear it, and looked up to the starry night. The fourteen stars of the Wheel burned clearly at zenith, telling him nothing.

"Obas Limm was am old mam, whem I was borm," continued M'rongovorth. "He lived im Yathar, several humdred kilometers from Tamsavar Arema, a wise amd respected humam who lived im the *charras*-fashiom of the Teachers of Cheltam. He, his wives, his childrem, all the livestock, all of us lived together im one huge room.

"As a Teacher he taught the Cheltam way to all who would listem—amd I was always there to listem. Though he seemed a poor mam, he also had a Screemer which received tape transmissioms directly from Tamsavar Cemtral Library. With it he taught lamguage to the smaller childrem, mathematics, history, literature, all the ramge of humam kmowledge, to the older omes.

"Thus I learmed too, though mo ome was aware."

From somewhere among the winding paths between the huts came a vagrant whiff of Djelgarth pine smoke. Man and bisfas paused to see if someone were coming.

Reassured, Jonnath spoke. "But—to learn in solitude like that? From my own experience I know the essence of the learning process is in the stress of question and answer, where the student learns from *interaction* with his teacher."

Bisfas lips curled in an alien smile, and M'rongovorth spoke gently.

"I told you I was a gemius, evem for ome of your race. Those reality relatiomships that humam studemts had to puzzle out with careful questioms, to me were obvious omce Obas Limm had demomstrated them the first time."

Now Jonnath smiled. "Okee. I'll believe it even if I can't accept it . . ."

"Why mot?" The bisfas sounded astonished, and his long thick tail lashed slowly from side to side as if with impatience. "Had I beem borm elsewhere, would I them have sought out a teacher? I thimk it possible—amd others may well have dome so before me. What happems to am imtelligemt mutatiom borm amomg a species with am Imtelligemce Factor of less tham 100, is up to chamce —amd to himself Chamce gave me Obas Limm."

"How intelligent are you, then?" Jonnath asked.

"A humam gemius might reach an Imtelligemce Factor of a thousamd, with average imtelligemce at approximately 450. I suspect mime is over 1200." The bisfas rumbled apologetically. "I would mot like you tho thimk I am a braggart . . ."

139

Jonnath chuckled, then asked, "But how did you come here?"

M'rongovorth's tail ceased lashing as he spoke. "One day I realized that Obas Linn was dying, and at a time when his humans were elsewhere I spoke to him at last. A wise and holy man indeed, he did not question what seemed to him a simple miracle.

"For that last week I spoke to him for hours every day, and learned of things he had not taught of. We spoke, finally, of what would become of me after his death, and at last agreed that though the Cheltan-Way was not for me, its teachings of the natural harmonics of life, which I had learned, dictated that I await what was to come. We became Cheltan-brothers then, and he died contented, peacefully."

A thought struck Jonnath, and it irritated him that he had not come up with it earlier. "Why me? I mean, why did you decide to announce yourself to me in particular? I presume you haven't spoken to anyone else since then?"

"Ah," said M'rongovorth. "Obas Linn died five Standard months ago. His family was poor, and sold me to the Arena to haul for the Star Games. Since then I have simply wandered about—they seldom pen up bisfas beasts because they are so docile and tame there is no need to—and waited for what would happen."

"But why *me?*"

"I knew of the conspiracy of your fellow Kalvaran. I knew that if I spoke to a Kalvaran I would somehow be brought into it—consider the advantages of someone like me on your side in a war of conspiracy!—and I did not like the sound of it, any more than you did."

"So that's it! And when you heard me tell them I was determined to go my own way, you figured you could trust me not to betray you to them."

"I knew already you were an excellent fighter, and your words were those of a man of more than average intelligence. I was growing bored here, and . . ."

Then Jonnath laughed. "But—this is really wonderful! What a pair of allies we'd make! You know I plan to Fight Free when the High Games begin—I'll buy you somehow afterward, and we'll go in search of my enemies!"

M'rongovorth gave a ghastly alien chuckle. "Very well,

my friemd. But you must do certaim things for me as well . . ."

Jonnath frowned. "Within reason, but what?"

M'rongovorth wheezed his strange sigh. "There is much I do not mow. Obtaim for me a Screemer and tapes— mamy tapes, as mamy as you cam possibly mamage. You search for revenge amd advemture, while I, I search for advemture—amd mowledge."

"Done!" said Jonnath with delight. "What a pair of heroes *we* will make!"

The High Games of Tansavar focused the attention of three quarters of the planetary population onto its arena. Only Kinkaid's Star World, and Zarmith II itself, could boast of a show so rich and bloody with pageantry, death, skill, and savagery. Hence to the billion plus audience on Tansavar was added twenty billion more from the hundreds of systems ruled by the Star Guards of Zarmith II.

Jonnath was acutely aware of this—and of its essential irrelevance to him as he stood alone on the sandy floor of the arena.

Popular belief was that no man in the arena knew what he was to face on any day. It was all supposed to be extempore, no one having a chance to prepare a battle plan beforehand. Aesthetic theorists held that this preserved the basic purity of the artform, which was survival.

But Jonnath knew that it generally made little difference to a professional who or what he would be matched against; by the time he had progressed to the point of being justifiably confident in his abilities, he was prepared to face anything he had faced before.

He cursed to himself. The sun was stronger than he'd known it in Changar. The packed crowds observed his loneliness impassively. The sun that beat upon him was blocked from them; they watched in cool contentment as the sweat beaded slowly on his breech-clouted figure and rolled along his deeply tanned skin.

That sly look on Pitmaster Ishau's face when he had hinted that his first assignment in Fighting Free of the High Games would be relatively simple—a Karshon winged slug . . . there was no reason he shouldn't have been told, Jonnath thought to himself. Ishau knew he had a method for handling the monsters that was simple, yet pleased the crowds with its graceful unexpectedness.

Then why that sly chuckle from Ishau?

"Excellencies of the Hundred Cities," came the softly echoing boom of the annunciator, "a man to watch stands before you—Jonnath of Kallor, who has declared for Fighting Free in the first week of the High Games. This morning, he opens his fourteen trials against a winged Karshonite. This specimen was shipped in from Karshon yesterday. Your attention, excellencies: prospects of a most entertaining combat! A ten minute spectacle; the man must win in less than five to continue in his fight for freedom."

Yesterday! Jonnath heard nothing more from the annunciator after that word—the Karshonite had not been offworld long enough for its poison sacs to have been neutralized!

So much for Ishau's chuckle—he had sent him out to fight a beast whose venom was the most feared poison in the known regions of the two galaxies! *I've fought those jords more than twenty times, and never escaped without a scratch yet,* Jonnath thought, and added grimly, *Obviously they don't like gladiators to Fight Free . . .*

One slight wound meant death unless the poison had passed that critical point, about thirty hours offworld, and had already broken down.

There was no time to curse now, no time to worry, plan, or regret his decision to Fight Free, no time to retch with the sick fear that had stricken him, no time to convulse with terror like the fresh ears he suddenly felt— the great ponderous doors to the animal pits were swinging open . . .

The arena was silent for a time. Beyond the gaping doors lay unbroken blackness.

Then from the depths of the animal pits came a sickening buzz—the beating of the million-clawed wings of the Karshonite slug!

There was a blurred glitter at the gate to the pit; the crowd murmured then in an indistinguishable babble. It was against even the traditions of the Star Guard arenas to send anyone out against a Karshonite whose poison was still live.

They all know that, he realized, *and they know I know*

*it. And we all know that none of us knows for certain
if the poison still has its virulence . . . Dom clever.*
The thought was infinitely bitter.

Could he take a chance that the poison was now inactive? From his past experience there didn't appear to be much choice . . .

The winged slug hovered in the gateway, then spiraled slowly upward to the roof of the arena.

It beat its head against the clear dome for a time, its small brain baffled by the simple illusion, then spiraled back down slowly.

On the way down its attention was caught by the scarlet dais at which sat a dozen or so Zarmithan nobles. The slug's buzzing accelerated to a shrill whine, and it darted toward the splash of color.

Baffled by the forcefence, its shrill whining sharper, harsher, the slug swooped lower—and caught sight of the lone figure on the dazzling white sands.

The trick old Yissor had taught him wouldn't work today. He'd never used any other—lure the slug into flying directly at him level with the ground, fake it into veering upward by jumping upward—then drop to the ground and stab his short dagger into the brain center in the monster's throat.

It wouldn't work now because it invariably meant at least a slight injury, since the slug would take several seconds to die and would still try desperately to savage anything near it even as it died. One can recover from wounds, was Yissor's philosophy.

But not from Karshon poison . . .

Scant seconds to plan now—he had only one chance to choose a course of action, and he had to assume the poison was still active.

The slug approached Jonnath slowly, at an angle, some three meters above his head. He knew it was the search pattern, and held fast.

Wild, unused to attacking intelligent beings, the slug hesitated, then dropped lower and circled Jonnath at some ten meters distant, level with his head.

With its own kind of wiliness, it veered away as if convinced Jonnath was not prey. Its buzzing whine dropped back down the scale to almost normal—

—and then it reversed its path and streaked just above

the ground toward Jonnath, at twice its previous speed! Its meter long repulsive body quivered with eagerness.

Three years' living at what for him was approximately one-half normal gravity had cut down on his native Kalvar advantages. But Jonnath had kept in shape, and the last month here at Tansavar among other Kalvaran had provided him with additional incentive to sharpen his waning advantage.

Thus when the slug was almost upon him he leaped upward a full meter and a half, clearing the Karshonite's segmented head with half a meter to spare—and dropped down solidly on the jellylike midbody of the slug . . . a hundred and fifteen kilos of dead weight concentrated in the horny heels of his feet.

It was a weaponless kill, and the audience went into paroxysms of applause . . .

That afternoon they took the small knife from him and issued him a long double-edged sword. Pitmaster Ishau clapped him on the shoulder heartily, and said, "After this morning, they're all with you out there, so I'd be a fool to send you against certain death. Before, they expected that. Now they're waiting to watch you win—but you'll have to win with style, or they'll cancel your freedom like that. You've got a good shot at winning it all, lad, but you'll have to win it big, with a flourish, or they'll see you back here next week."

Jonnath grinned coldly. "No tricks, eh? Except perhaps a bear-wolf insane on newcoke, or a professional with a double needle of bright-black, right?"

The Pitmaster's smile was quite pleasant. "Only if you start looking bad . . ."

In the month he'd been at Tansavar, the audiences had learned that he could kill an armed man in two minutes with his bare hands. This afternoon, then, he was given a sword—against five armed professionals, two of them Kalvaran.

As he stood once more on the hot bright sands waiting for the annunciator to finish, he realized that he was drained of emotion. Nothing was left except what always remained—the pure problem of simple survival.

No, not simply survival, he knew, but survival with that grand gesture that would hold the ever-wavering emotions of the vast beast that now fixed its million eyes upon him and his five antagonists.

Survival was simple.

Success was not.

By the time the annunciator clicked off, Jonnath had it worked out in his mind. Instantly on the attack, he closed with one of the Kalvaran and dispatched him after one brief engagement of blades. The crowd roared.

Supposing he would play cat and krol with them, the remaining four were momentarily taken aback with this maneuver.

Wresting the dead man's sword from his lax grasp, Jonnath tossed it to the remaining Kalvaran.

"Two swords, fresh ears—try to last longer than *he* did," Jonnath shouted, knowing that every sound on the arena floor carried throughout the entire stadium.

The Kalvaran backed away warily, holding the two swords awkwardly—as Jonnath had expected, he was not used to two weapons. But under the circumstances he could hardly discard the unwanted one; it would seem to him an advantage to have it.

As the Kalvaran hesitated, the other three darted in front of him, attempting the glory of halting Jonnath's bid for freedom themselves.

Unused to fighting in unison, however, they got in each other's way almost immediately. So it was a moment later that Jonnath darted under the hasty thrust of one of the smaller men, knocked his weapon away, and picked him up bodily.

Effortlessly Jonnath tossed the squirming body at one of the other two, who managed to spit the body on his sword while trying not to. Moving swiftly, Jonnath engaged with the man while he was still trying to free his blade, and swiftly broke his neck with a blow of his free hand, keeping his own blade free.

Now Jonnath's Kalvaran opponent stepped in front of the remaining smaller man and raised his two swords menacingly. Unwilling to lose his chance at fame, the smaller man unexpectedly jostled the Kalvaran aside, and sprang at Jonnath.

In a moment Jonnath dispatched him, and faced the remaining Kalvaran.

Jonnath drove the point of his sword deeply into the

145

shimmering white sands in front of him, and said, "I will not use my sword again this day." The audience, whose cheers had been increasing with each death, went mad with applause for a moment—then fell deathly silent.

The Kalvaran advanced at a tangent, reminding Jonnath of the Karshon slug's search pattern. In turn, Jonnath circled the blade quivering in the sand, and faced the Kalvaran.

Two long narrow blades darted past the hilt; Jonnath dodged left, then right as the blades followed him and banged against the standing sword!

The interruption of the swordsman's rhythmic patterns was all Jonnath needed; before the other could recover he was on him, knocking the swords from his hands with paralyzing blows from his clenched fists.

The crowd roared like a lion paralyzing its intended kill as Jonnath lifted the man over his head. The annunciator could barely be heard above the waves of sound.

"The verdict," Jonnath heard at last, "is death for Habar Tor, and all possessions of all five men defeated by Jonnath to go to him!"

There was the usual festival Outside, that night. Tarshia, the Blue from Abbess, danced her ritual celebration for winning her fight in the arena that day. A crowd of young nobility from Zarmith II itself, here for the High Games, yelled and stamped on the packed earth of the courtyard, urging her on.

Jonnath sat at the edge of the large center area, sipping at a mild wine and smoking a Merry. He felt vaguely depressed, even though he had discovered that Habar Tor was worth over ten thousand dahls, all of which—less a prudent percentage to Ishau the Pitmaster—had been transferred to him. The other four had less than a thousand between them; *it all makes a nice beginning,* he thought, *if I can just make it to the end . . .*

"May we exchange palms, Jonnath?" He looked up. Willan stood there. A few paces away was Adalph.

He nodded, extending his two hands, and the other clasped them. Jonnath indicated Willan should sit, then gestured to Adalph.

An autoclang began playing the click music of Lim, as he and Adalph exchanged hands; Adalph sat and spoke.

146

"You were good today—very good. We can still use your help, you know. And perhaps we did not act quite fairly with you."

"You were uncertain about us," said Willan. "We should have told you what our plan was—and who brought it to us."

"Who?" Jonnath frowned. "I hardly see what—"

It was Adalph's turn to gesture. Another tall Kalvaran figure came forward.

For a moment Jonnath failed to recognize him.

Then—"Kilar! But you were traveling in the Zia Complex when Zarmith struck!"

His uncle Kilar Gri smiled humorlessly down at Jonnath. "Don't tell that to the Star Guards, lad. They might wonder to find me in one of their arenas . . ."

Adalph leaned toward Jonnath. "He brought us a message; this was the only sure way to get it through to us."

"It's a simple message, but we'll need everyone we can get to put it in effect. About six Standard months ago, the Emperor Shaikon III personally sent for me and several dozen other Kalvaran officials who had been abroad in the Ten Star Complex at the time of . . ." Kilar paused imperceptibly, then went on; the three other Kalvaran affected not to notice. "It seems that he has developed a weapon which, though not yet perfected, can now be used against Zarmith. And Shaikon's becoming desperate; although his possessions are several times greater than those of the Star Guards, his power is much weaker than his ancestors, and many of his nominally subject possessions have become so independent that they will not unite behind him to fight Zarmith's threat.

"Knowing of the rise of the Kalvaran as a professional class in themselves in many of the larger arenas, he has devised a plan to free us if we will bind ourselves to fight for him as an elite army.

"That is what we need men like you for, my brother's son. With some ten thousand fighting men here in Tansavar Arena alone, we need leaders—and you are a natural leader." Kilar Gri smiled again, but the warmth was all surface. "I am not trying to flatter you, Jonnath. I simply state the facts. Now, when you Fight Free, we lose your service. You see my point?"

Jonnath noted Kilar's apparent confidence that he

would win his remaining twelve fights, at the same time that he shook his head.

"No, I cannot serve two aims at once, my father's brother Kilar. I am sworn to vengeance for what was done to me and those I love—and to find Sheira. If I stay here and fight in your rebellion, I will never find my enemies—or Sheira. And I must; this is what sustains me in the arena. This is why I still try to survive when all around me swims in blood and death and terror."

Kilar stood. "Vengeance makes a lifetime bitter."

Jonnath shrugged, as Kilar went on. "Let me warn you, that the dangers are as great outside these stone walls as they are here. When Shaikon strikes with his weapon on the final day of the High Games, and we wreak *our* vengeance before departing, there will no longer be any safety anywhere within the Zarmith Empery for Kalvaran, slave or free . . ."

Pitmaster Ishau knew the crowd now favored Jonnath —and he knew the Kalvaran was prepared to be generous to him with his winnings. So it was that Jonnath seemed to face perils in his last twelve fights in Tansavar Arena, as great as any he had faced in the last three years. And so it was also that those professionals he fought, Earthish and Kalvaran, were men who had themselves amassed much money in their arena days. The crowds were vastly pleased with Jonnath's victories, and awarded him invariably with all possessions of the defeated . . . and twenty percent of those winnings went to Pitmaster Ishau.

Over the last fight, however, Ishau had no real control. For as tradition dictated, Jonnath had to be sent out, fresh ears naked, against a man armed with a weapon he had faced but once before . . .

It was the hottest day so far. Gouts of fire from the crude oil flamethrower speared into the sands around him, and smoked blackly in dank pools spotting the gritty whiteness.

It was with a thrill of exhilaration that he realized his opponent was no arena-wise Yissor, old in his trade of death, but was young and relatively new to his professional specialty.

Why, he hadn't even tried to deceive Jonnath about the range and frequency of his weapon! And his attempts to anticipate where Jonnath would dodge were guesswork.

It was only a matter of a pair of minutes before Jonnath closed with the man, wrested the flamethrower from him, and raised him over his head.

"Death! Death!" the crowd roared. "Freedom for Jonnath!"

Finally the ennunciator could be heard over the cheers of the audience. "Freedman Jonnath, you have heard the verdict of the audience. Dilliw Ourn is to die."

Jonnath set his opponent down, and whispered fiercely into his ear, "Kneel, man, if you hope to live!"

With his victim kneeling in the sand before him, Jonnath shouted, struggling to be heard. Presently an announciator mike swiveled out over the arena to pick up his words, and the crowd quieted.

"I crave one gift," he cried into the mike, and his words reverberated through the vast arena. "If I have fought well here and pleased you, let this man beside me live too. I would leave the arena as I joined it—sparing the life of my opponent!"

The appeal pleased the crowd, and it went wild once more as its hero strode for the last time from the arena— side by side with the man he had defeated . . .

7 Priest of the Mad God

HE REALIZED he hadn't thought it out fully, by the afternoon of his first day of freedom in the city of Tansavar.

He was famous.

Everywhere he went, on the back of the magnificently caparisoned bisfas beast everyone knew he had bought from the arena as one last gesture of freedom, everywhere the people knew him.

He had Fought Free and garnered almost two hundred thousand dahls in the process. He was the most famous fighting man from Tansavar Arena since the captive Valakh hero, Garoth, carved out his legend a century and more ago. He was hailed on every street by beggars and Star Guards, laborers and princes of Zarmith, children and beautiful women and aged men.

Jonnath and M'rongovorth traveled down the wide avenues, under the giant ferns artificially kept alive, their fronds waving in the richly oxygenated air that Tansavar was celebrated for. The pungent scent of the djurga, a flowering vine that wrapped around the giant ferns and lived in symbiosis with them, became stronger as they reached an intersection with an even broader avenue.

The streets were filled with darting, buzzing jeefs, both large and small. Their ground effect fans kept the air in a constant stir, and Jonnath's crisp blue cape fluttered almost constantly.

Fresh from what seemed to him like a lifetime in the arena pits, he breathed the alien scents and absorbed the alien vibrations in the air. Kalvar soil, climate, and atmosphere was not suited for the symbiotic ferns and djurga, and vehicles in Kallor had been almost entirely the new magnetic craft introduced a generation ago from another Vegan colony, The Happies, a three-planet system. Those craft had been silent; Jonnath found the high whine of the jeefs took some getting used to.

Above them, the city skies were full of many-colored floaters, swooping and sailing in a holiday dance pattern that was intoxicating to follow.

With three weeks still to come in the High Games, the city was a magnet for the planetary population; and thousands of offworlders had arrived for the festivities. Here and there were other gladiators, also in blue cloaks. They, like Jonnath, were men who had Fought Free from various arenas in the past, men who were now drawn to the High Games by obscure urges they themselves seemed unsure about.

There were even rare true aliens from Q'amrat on the far side of the galaxy—red-skinned oxygen breathers a meter in height who looked like nothing so much as tiny pyramids on thin stilts.

And wherever Jonnath and M'rongovorth wandered, there came the hails from passersby, the endless instant recognition.

After several hours, Jonnath turned the bisfas into a large park area, where giant ferns gave way to a stand of neo-oak. At the far side of the park the trees thinned away, giving them a view of the proud towers of Tansavar rising in the near distance behind them. The park was only sparsely populated; they could talk without being overheard.

M'rongovorth uttered his ghastly sighing chuckle. "A bit more tham you expected, eh, boss?"

Jonnath ignored the meaningless archaichism; he'd become used to the delight the bisfas took in displaying his knowledge of earlier forms of Standard. "How can I find out anything when everyone is going to crowd around me like that? Why, they hang on everything I say! I cannot ask the thronging multitudes the whereabouts of Krith Vaggar and the rest, can I?"

"Quite true, Jommath," the bisfas agreed. "I cam omly see ome possibility—amd it will take time, more time perhaps tham you wish to take."

"I suppose it was foolish of me to think I could find anything on the first day. Still, I have the feeling it would be best to do what I can quickly, before that fool Shaikon's plan starts up."

"There is omly ome way, them, Jommath; the people must tire of you. You must be so much among them that they stop paying attemtiom to you. After that . . . you will be able to speak quietly to whomever you wish."

"Mmm." he muttered, thinking. "I suppose so, friend. It'll be a little rough on you, though, carrying me around everywhere, eh?"

"Mot at all; I too desire to see the sights of Tamsavar. It is importamt that you mot be too impatiemt, that is all . . ."

And so they left the park and reentered the golden city of Tansavar.

Again he was hailed at every turn when they caught sight of the massive shambling bisfas with the blue-caped giant sitting in its saddle.

"That's it!" Jonnath realized, trying to keep his lips from moving so that people wouldn't think he was a mental defective, talking to his bisfas. "It's this dom blue cape they gave me for Fighting Free. Everyone recognizes it—so they recognize me. From a distance I'd be just another starfoot, without it."

"Take it off," M'rongovorth rumbled, as quietly as he could. "Do you have to talk so much?"

"If I take it off, some will still recognize me, and they'll wonder about it. The last thing I want is people wondering what I'm up to. And what do you care about me talking to you so much?"

"Because I have this feelimg that humam beimgs might just be a little prejudiced agaimst am imtelligemt beimg that's five times their size. Okay?"

"Okee, M'rongo. We'll keep down the consultations in public."

Now Jonnath and M'rongovorth turned into another wide street. No giant ferns lined the Avenue of Temples, along whose five kilometer length the hieretic buildings of fifty strange religions soared, squatted, sprawled, or stood quietly in rapt contemplative peace.

Jonnath remembered his father's views on the proliferation of religions over the last thousand years. Telvar Gri held that the tenuous interconnections of ten thousand separate governments, empires, kingdoms, and republics teeming in the galaxy were being strained past the breaking point by the new efforts to cross and conquer the intergalactic gulfs. But the rise of new religions, in what many were calling the Era of Proselytism, tended to knit the shifting cultures back together to a considerable extent. Jonnath had never fully accepted his father's views, but even here on Tansavar, one of the home worlds of the Zarmithan Empire, the government sanctioned all religions who desired it, as if instinctively recognizing their overarching importance for the human race.

Here stood the kilometer high twin spiral towers of the Nongri-shomuth, bannered by ten thousand flags of the planets honoring them. Next to the twin spiral, the looming translucent cube of the Kalimanitarj, symbolizing the perception of ultimate reality that came to Anitarj the Founder, on the planet Kalim.

A considerable distance beyond was the freeform concrete structure of the Most Feared—Daggoth, The Mad God. Eternally the shrieks of the doomed insane echoed within the meaningless convolutions of the temple. Nothing stood near it; it was shunned in spirit as in reality. Nor did people pass nearby it; floaters did not inspect it from the sky as they did the other temples.

Only the Believers of Daggoth came there, the Shunned Ones, the Feared servants of the Most Feared.

Elsewhere on the Avenue of Temples stood the sacred

monuments of the Twelve Gods, the buried Pantheon of The Eld, the Golden Pyramid, the Mirror of Chang, the Hall of Mysteries, the Dream Palace of Risha, to Jonnath all a nightmare pilgrimage through the insane racial mind of mankind's attempts to find mistaken paths to reality among the aimless patterns of its history among the stars along the multiwave paths.

"Do the bisfas beasts have anything like religion, M'rongo?" Jonnath reached down and scratched a shaggy triangular ear.

"Mmmph," the bisfas muttered. "How should I mow? Stupid amimals—I mever learmed their lamguage, if they had one. Culturally speakimg, I'm a humam beimg just like you. As for me, I prefer philosophy to religiom, if you must mow. I fimd the smell of priestly imcemse distasteful, amd for me to bow for am absolutiom is am absurdity I prefer mot to imdulge myself im . . ."

Jonnath chuckled appreciatively. "You old scoundrel! If you're a sinner, your sins must be gigantic!"

"If I'm a simmer, I'm a humgry ome." And the bisfas turned off the Avenue of Temples at the next intersection.

"Do you suppose," M'rongovorth continued, "that we cam fimd a place at which we cam both feed?"

"Ordinarily, no. But we're not ordinary, are we! Do you think their ferry will be able to lift you to that floater restaurant up there?" Jonnath indicated a huge translucent flying plaza, as big as the city square of park that lay underneath it. Several smaller floaters were carrying patrons up and down.

"It *should* hold me, Jommath. But will they—"

One of the ferry platforms was resting on the blue green park grass, waiting for customers; several were already aboard, but there was space for at least thirty more.

"Bardinet's, at your service," said an orange-cloaked attendant. "Ah, it is Jonnath the Free! Master Bardinet will be well pleased that you desire to eat here!"

"Good. Then it will not distress him that I do not wish to be separated from my faithful companion here." Arrogantly Jonnath slapped his korgaleather boots against the bisfas' sides, urging him forward relentlessly onto the ferry platform.

The orange-cloaked attendant shuddered, and a shadow

153

of pained irritation touched his face, which was absolutely hairless in the manner of the Alexeites. He stepped over to the ferry controls, and presently the platform lurched upward, narrowly missing a passing one man sled.

Night and day, Bardinet's hung at from fifteen to twenty-five stories above the patch of parkland, providing a commanding view of the westerly side of Tansavar City.

The arrival of the bisfas beast on Bardinet's caused a considerable flurry. Knowing the large quantity of money Jonnath had won in his last heroic week in the arena, however, the staff did not protest his eccentricity, and eventually they were led to a spot near the edge.

"Say," whispered Jonnath when, for a moment, no one was near, "what do you eat, anyway?"

"Do mot laugh, Jommath . . . potato pamcakes? With sour cream?"

Jonnath smiled but did not say anything. M'rongovorth eyed him with a hurt look, and turned his head away. Soon Jonnath was seated at a low table, M'rongovorth lying on the floor beside him like some nightmare dog out of the medieval hell of the Twenty-fifth Century.

An elderly man dressed all in deep blue velvet approached them with a sheet of some gleaming substance. Jonnath took the blank sheet, then saw that when he focused his eyes upon it, it became simply a menu. He handed it back with a large gesture of indifference, and said, "Bring me the best you have—that's not all prettied up past recognition for the would-be connoisseurs."

The elderly man bowed, then indicated the bisfas beast, lolling casually by the table and looming over it.

"Him?" said Jonnath, "oh, just start bringing him potato pancakes—and sour cream—until he stops eating 'em. And plenty of water, I suppose. Don't worry, he's housebroken . . ."

The waiter bowed again, still impassive, and strode away. Far from impassive, the people at nearby tables were turning to study the eccentricities of this Jonnath the Free. He paid no attention to them, but concentrated on the landscape of Tansiavar as it was displayed to him, sitting at the verge of the platform. Thus it was that he became aware that the platform was slowly rotating.

"I hope the motion doesn't get you airsick, old friend," he said to the bisfas. Was it his imagination or was

M'rongovorth irritated? Oh, well, at least people might start getting used to him talking to what they must assume was simply a mute animal.

The meal was magnificent; it took four waiters in powder-blue to arrange it properly in front of him. There were twelve dishes in all, none large enough for a meal in itself, but artistically balanced with the others for total culinary effect. He had the blue velvet headwaiter explain the unfamiliar dishes.

"This is dawn-phase Changeling breast, from Altairion. This, inch-thick strips of the skin of the giant Kinkaid's Star World spice ant. That, fresh bisfas tongue from Cindy —the forage on that world adds an incomparable flavor to the meat. The central dish, of course, is a rarity, but you asked for the best—rare steak of beef, from the cow, imported at great expense from Earth itself. The soups and vegetables . . ."

Jonnath nodded his approval. Another waiter came up with a small floatercart filled with bottles of chilled wines. Jonnath indicated that the headwaiter should choose that which would go best with the feast, and a small green bottle with a narrow neck was placed in front of him.

"From Fayal, sir. It is nonalcoholic, but its delicate flavor is perfect for complementing such a meal. And if you wish added enhancement, we have several highly refined cannabis compounds, and—"

Jonnath waved the elderly headwaiter away with another large gesture. "I am sure nothing could improve on this."

The waiter bowed deferentially once more.

Two other waiters appeared with a floatercart piled high with fresh hot potato pancakes, which they laid out on a large mat in front of the bisfas. M'rongovorth snorted with approval.

Two weeks had passed, and only one week remained in the High Games, when Jonnath sat beside an unsavory figure at an open air narcotics bar. A few steps away at the curb stood M'rongovorth, munching on some stringy vines.

"Information about certain Star Guards, is it," said the shabby man, who had a scar running from his left ear straight across to his nose. "And why should you be wanting to know about Star Guards, eh? They look after their own, you know. They're none too popular, even in the home worlds they've made so fat and prosperous, and they know it well. Vengeance, I suppose?"

The man blinked up at the setting sun, then wheezed and continued, "Can't we go inside to discuss this? Dom light hurt my eyes . . ."

"No," said Jonnath, "there's nobody else out here on the streetside this afternoon. I prefer the anonymous open air to wretched little rooms . . . with hidden fixtures in the walls."

"Hee-hee," Scarface cackled, "if I was planning to scrag you to the lobsters, I'd have had a couple beam mikes on you the moment you spoke to me!" He wiped a dirty square of cloth over his oily, sweating forehead.

"Very well. I want to know about a Star Guard captain who took part in the . . . attack . . . on Kalvar. His name is Vaggar. I suspect he is the same Krith Vaggar who has some connection with the mysterious Lady Tza."

"Is . . . it . . . so . . ." The scar lifted slightly as the man smiled without humor. "For additional information on that one, I give you special price—twice what I would ordinarily charge. And who are the others, Mightiness?"

"The members of his squad then. I have three names: Borlat, Liathas, and Bressan. I especially want Borlat. There will be another member of the squad that you cannot locate—Zelavan Gannit. I killed him myself some months ago in Tansavar Arena."

Scarface scratched a shaggy grey eyebrow. "Dom, but you get around! Anyone else?"

Jonnath hesitated. "It doesn't seem likely that you can find the others I'm interested in. I don't even know their names. Vaggar was on a routine patrol, however; these others were on a specific detail the first day of the attack— to assassinate a number of Grand Counsellors in Kallor City. The patrol I want did get at least two—that I know of for certain, that is—Alhavan Tor and . . ." He realized he was out of breath, almost choking. From dark and deep within him, raw painful emotion was surging out

He paused and breathed deeply. Scarface's eyes peered curiously at him as he spoke again. "Alhavan Tor," he repeated firmly then, "and Telvar Gri, with his wife Eila. My parents," he added defiantly and unnecessarily.

Scarface nodded. All business now, he had taken out several slips of paper, and jotted cryptic notes.

Then, standing, he held out a dirty hand. "You paid a hundred just to talk to me. It'll be a thousand dahl now; I'll start digging. Then it will be two thousand for each positive identification and certification of present location. Fair?" He grinned humorlessly.

"No," said Jonnath grimly, "but I'll pay it." He stood, keyed his chest wallet with his thumbprint, and counted out ten worn squares of bright green plastic. "Don't come to my quarters; I'll be here every evening at the same time."

He walked away from his untouched drink—Scarface stretched out a bony arm and tossed it down casually—and pretended to kick M'rongovorth.

"Up, you lazy putridity," Jonnath shouted, "take me away from this place of vileness!"

A few minutes later, as the bisfas carried Jonnath down a wide avenue, M'rongovorth said with irritation in his hoarse low voice, "Why the productiom about me beimg am amimal. Evem a real bisfas might have feelimgs, you mow."

"Listen, M'rongo, you eat and drink and share the same sleeping quarters with me. You don't want to be found out for what you are, and I want to avoid being found out for what I am not—a pit-trained sexual deviant. They know every sin and shame here, and, while I'm sinning a little here and there, I'd prefer to be known for real, not imagined, shames."

The bisfas uttered his complaining laugh.

Scarface—in the intervening two days Jonnath had taken some trouble to establish that his name was Ligario Gargano—had a sly grin on his face.

"I have first, the six names and present locations you asked me for. But of course you will wish to pay me the twelve thousand for these identifications?" Money passed, and Ligario resumed.

"Zelavan Gannit, of course, sleeps in the bellies of the bellies of the scavenger krols out by the arena. Captain Krith Vaggar travels with the Lady Tza—and will be with her tomorrow when she arrives at her palace from Zarmith.

"Bressan Toogey was killed in the action at Starcross Station last year. He was still on Death Patrol. Tigierol Vanjis, called Liathas, was commissioned a lieutenant shortly after the Rape of Kalvar—" Here Ligario paused and licked his lips, a sneer on his face.

"Vangis commands a scoutship with the fleet near Starcross. Ah! You are unhappy? He is a Star Guard . . . and he is star-guarding!" Ligario chuckled. "And Vinko Phoral and Nortresh Jemz serve under him."

Jonnath scowled. "There is one more name."

Ligario laughed and mopped his forehead. "Have you seen the Avenue of Temples yet, mighty fighter?"

Jonnath clenched his fist, then slammed it down on the table between them. It shook with the blow, and Ligario winced away. "Do not play these dangerous games with me, you frail imitation of a man. What is it to you that I have seen the temples?"

"Why, that if you have, you have passed quite close to him whom you seek—Borlat Vorz."

"How is that?" Jonnath asked, holding himself in check with an effort.

"Oh, now, well, some months ago, you must know, struck by the shamefulness of the life he had led—a vastly evil man, my lord—he cast his cloak."

"He became a *priest?*" Jonnath was amazed.

Ligario's smile was not comforting. "A priest, yes. An invincible Star Guard no longer, he performs the most humbling duties, ministering to the insane . . .

"Borlat Vorz is a priest of the Most Feared—Daggoth, The Mad God!"

Jonnath's money long since safely hidden on him, Ligario allowed himself to smile even more broadly at the tall strong figure seated opposite him, obviously struggling to control his anger.

"You do not like my manner, noble one," said Ligario in a soft unpleasant voice. "But I remind that I have seven *other* names for you, my lord . . . you have the other fourteen thousand dahls?"

Money changed hands once more. "Well then," said Ligario, standing and pushing his bench back, "the other names you seek, the patrol that assassinated your father and mother: Krith Vaggar, Borlat Vorz, Zelavan Gannit, Bressan—"

Ligario jumped backward swiftly, avoiding the grasp of the pair of huge hands that reached out for him.

"Do not mock me, filth," hissed Jonnath. "Don't make a game of my vengeance."

Something dark was in Ligario's hand. "This is a Nangee flasher; you're fresh ears if you take another step toward me. I don't mock vengeance, Free One—I've taken mine, and more than once.

"I don't know why you're so surprised, but Vaggar's patrol is the one you want, the *only* one you want. The facts are as I gave them to you. Now you will kindly stand *precisely* where you are, while I proceed on my way . . ."

Carefully watching Jonnath, Ligario sidled off, then darted into an open doorway. There was a heavy metallic *clang* immediately after, as the door slammed behind the little man with the scar.

The sun had almost set past the translucent cube of the Kalimanitarj when M'rongovorth came to a halt in front of the freeform Temple of the Most Feared: Daggoth, The Mad God.

There was little direct light on the concrete; Jonnath became aware that the entire surface of the temple was becoming alive with a myriad of swirling colors.

"Obviously phosphors, mixed in with the concrete at the time of construction," he said, looking up at the eight gates, each a different size and shape.

"Amd as it gets dark . . . a most imposimg sight, my friemd."

With the onset of twilight, the two heard odd noises coming from inside the temple of the Mad God—resembling human voices, but raised to a pitch of frenzy unnatural by some supernal force.

"Is it laughter . . . or agony?" Jonnath found the eerie screams unsettling—especially as the sounds were growing louder. He eased the Cheul pistol he had recently purchased out of its magnetic holster, and with his other hand loosened his sword in its scabbard.

"Jommath, I thimk I will go with you imside the temple. It does mot soumd as safe as Tamsavar Arema. I thimk that door over there, secomd from the left, will fit me micely."

"I won't argue . . ."

The darkly cavernous openings proved to have no gates, no bars, no restraints of any kind. They proceeded inside, the human with sword drawn and Cheul pistol locked on open fire.

"Faugh! Smells like carrion of the arena before the krols have settled in and done their cleansing. It's obvious Daggoth is not a spirit of the waters . . ."

A voice boomed behind them. "As ye have not entered in the prescribed manner, I perceive ye are not of the faith of the Most Feared. What would you in this temple, then, consecrated as it is to the holy madnesses?"

"I seek a priest of—"

"You seek vengeance. Your soul reeks of it. Know that here in this temple, your vengeance has been negated. I will let you see and speak with the former Borlat Vorz, but you must set all your weapons aside."

His eyes now accustomed to the gloomy darkness, Jonnath saw they were in an antechamber. He turned, and saw a tall man behind him—as tall as he was, but unnaturally slender, almost hollow in his spectral thinness.

"I will not ask how you know my mission, Old One," Jonnath said, using the customary mode of addressing an unknown priest. "I will set aside my weapons . . . and leave Borlat Vorz as I find him."

"Very well," said the reed-thin figure. "Follow me."

Jonnath set his weapons on a shelf, while M'rongovorth pressed up closely behind him, as if to remind him not to leave him behind. Absently he scratched the beast on the head and wondered why he had foresworn vengeance on the murderer so easily.

The priest led them through wide doorways through several large unoccupied chambers similar to the one they had first entered, then halted at a barred door. Mad screams echoed through the corridors behind them. The priest spoke through the bars.

"Clouded Eye, a man is here to speak with you who came with bitter vengeance in his heart. I dispense you from your ministrations, for the time that you spend discoursing with him. Come forth, Clouded Eye . . ."

The door swung open, and a foul stench Jonnath had already noticed became stronger. A hooded figure stood in the doorway. Behind him several naked figures were

160

visible, prisoners in the small stone cell. They wailed softly.

"You are . . . were . . . Borlat Vorz?" asked Jonnath. He realized he was shaking with the conflict of many emotions.

The figure in the doorway cast his hood back over his bent shoulders and peered upward at Jonnath. One eye was missing from its socket; the other was partially filmed over. *A cataract,* thought Jonnath, *and a bad one. But that could be fixed in fifteen minutes . . . why does he bear it?*

"I have been Clouded Eye since I entered this holy place six months ago, tall strange one," the figure answered, then closed the door behind him, carefully throwing a huge bolt to hold it. The wailing increased to mad howling. "Come, let us sit in the main temple, and we shall speak together."

The thin priest had departed. M'rongovorth followed the two humans down a wide passageway and through a tall archway.

The main temple was large enough for several hundred. It was furnished with nothing but rows of plain backless benches. The walls were a solid frieze of carved faces wrenched with the agonies of infinite madnesses.

At the front of the main temple was an open space. On a slightly raised platform sat a large sphere of some polished black material, at least two meters in diameter.

"It is the symbol of Daggoth," said Borlat Vorz as the two sat down. M'rongovorth stood near them, quietly.

As if on cue, the insane faces carved on the walls began to glow with the same phosphorescence as the outer walls. M'rongovorth uttered an involuntary cough, and shifted his weight uneasily. For the first time, Jonnath found himself really wondering about the beast's attitude toward human religions.

"The Tall Master spoke of vengeance in your heart," said Borlat Vorz, his voice almost a whisper. "You are the first who has come to speak to me. Who are you, and what was I shamed of to you?"

"The invasion of Kalvar. You were on a patrol under Krith Vaggar. I have been informed it was this patrol that assassinated my father and mother. Later, after the city was conquered, you were again on patrol when you shot down the sister of the girl I was to marry. You fired the shot personally, and it was you who took away the girl Sheira while your fellows clubbed me down and had me sent into the arenas, from which I have recently Fought Free."

Borlat Vorz nodded. "I killed over a hundred men, women, and children in Kallor. It was shortly after that when I first visited a temple of Daggoth, driven by obscure feelings I still have not quite comprehended. And half a year ago I cast my cloak, left the Star Guards, became a priest.

"Here I tend the mad husks of the tortured men who served as priests here before me, till they went mad; they wait in all the hells for death now. It is my duty to ease their bodies in all ways until the madness takes me away into my own sanctified punishment and final release."

Jonnath was shaken. The calm low whisper of Borlat Vorz showed no fear of the future, nor regret at the past.

The whisper resumed. "You are puzzled. You see me here serenely poised between a lifetime of evil and a fate full of ultimate pain and madness and horror. I cannot explain to you how this is. The Tall Master, did you recognize him?"

Jonnath shook his head.

"He once was Cholm Erwall, and owned the planet Rolfe IV. In one week, over a million people on the planet died of Karshon poison, introduced into the water supply . . ."

"But . . . but that was over fifty years ago. Cholm Erwall disappeared before he could be found!"

"He had thought to prove himself the ultimate nihilist, denying even the importance of life. But the weight of his deed overwhelmed him, and by devious means he came here. He has been Tall Master here for almost half the century."

"But you said all who become priests here go mad!"

"All is at the disposal of Daggoth. One day Cholm-Erwall-that-was will become Tall-Master-that-was, a screaming mad thing whimpering on the floor. His madness will last as long as his service here.

"As will mine, some day. It is this that causes our serenity of spirit, for we know that our time of cleansing is inevitable, and just, and complete!"

Jonnath passed his hand over his face. "I . . . I don't know if I comprehend all you imply. Certainly nothing I might do seems to me as terrible as what you face."

Borlat Vorz nodded. "The cost for what I have done is high. Is this all you wished to speak to me of?"

"I . . . cannot think. There was—"

"Your friend here would speak of something, then. Do not fear for your secret here." And Borlat Vorz reached out and patted M'rongovorth on the head.

The bisfas beast rumbled once, hesitantly, then spoke. "How you mow of me is puzzlimg. But my friemd Jommath forgets ome item of imformatiom Ligario Gargamo could mot provide—what became of the girl Sheira?"

"Who was she?" said the priest.

Jonnath spoke. "The girl you took away after shooting her sister. In the home of Telvar Gri, where four looters lay dead, on the second morning of your invasion."

"Ah. Krith Vaggar gave her to the Lady Tza, as he had promised. He always catered to pure power, and through her he has gained much power indeed. I fear he will never become Aware of the Truth of Daggoth."

"I do not think I shall give him time," said Jonnath grimly. "Do you know what became of Sheira after that?"

"You will do what you will do," said Borlat, "but remember that the Lady Tza is unapproachable. As one of the Shadow Princes of Zarmith, together with Tenmith and . . . others, she has her private company of Star Guards, fully armed with forcefields. As for the girl, she could have been established on any of the dozen and more planets where the Lady Tza keeps permanent households awaiting her pleasure. If the girl still lives, that is. I can tell you nothing more."

Jonnath rose, and stood uncertainly. "Then . . . I suppose there is nothing more for me to ask here. And nothing to be done . . ."

"Perhaps an offering to the Feared One, man with vengeance in your soul. Perhaps then Daggoth will seek to understand you and to save you from our fate . . ."

This is the strangest of all, thought Jonnath, as he brought out a square of green plastic from his chest wallet. *A thousand dahls, and I'm putting it into the hands of a man I once swore to track down and kill . . .*

From somewhere appeared the figure of Cholm Erwall.

"I thank you in the name of the Mad God, my friends," said the Tall Master. "If you have finished, I will show you the passage out so that Clouded Eye may return to his charges. Sir, you leave here a man who may live longer than you. Remember neither to envy him nor hate him, nor any of us who live in the way of the Most Feared. We each died on the day we committed our first betrayal of our own humanity. Here for a time we seem to live again.

"Go in peace."

The sun had long since set when Jonnath and M'rongovorth appeared in the main door of the Temple of Daggoth The Mad God. Jonnath looked about him with an abstracted expression as he prepared to mount the bisfas.

"There is nothing for me to do out here after all, my friend," he said, and hoisted himself into the saddle. "I might as well have stayed in the pits."

"I see omly two ways to reach the mysterious Lady Tza," observed M'rongovorth as he set off down the Avenue of Temples. "Form a free company of gladiators who have themselves Fought Free. Over three humdred of them are here to watch the High Games. I am sure half would follow you. Hire the free compamy imto her service. From them your course would be clear. Or, form the free company amd have them ready to move at your orders. Get im touch with your friemds im the arema—William, Kilar, Adaph. Aid them. Them perhaps they will aid *you* . . ."

"They are fools," muttered Jonnath. "What chance have they when they depend on a crack-grained lunatic who should have been disinherited before he could take his throne."

"A better chamce tham you do, Jommath. Amd if you do mot succeed om your owm before the High Games are over, it is likely that the Lady Tza *amd* her Krith Vaggar will depart whem the famcy seizes her. Umless your friemds im the arema succeed, of course . . ."

"Lunatics," said Jonnath once more, but his voice belied the word. "Counting on a weapon that probably does not exist."

8 Savage Noon

BUT the Emperor Shaikon III's weapon did exist. High above the translucent dome of Tansavar Arena on the last day of the High Games, a needle of flame appeared in the sky, then lanced downward at the dome and shattered its way through it . . .

With his small force of free gladiators, Jonnath awaited the arrival of the weapon. There was nothing to do but wait, after the hurried activity of the morning. He and M'rongovorth had hauled a large supply of Nangee flashers and Leeh rifles to the Outside, on the pretext of their being supplies for the great feast scheduled after the conclusion of the High Games.

He and his two hundred were to move only when the first stage of the attack was over and a prognosis of the situation could be made. Chafing at the inaction, Jonnath cursed slowly and steadily to himself, hardly realizing he was speaking.

A confusion of thoughts roiled through his mind, fatigued with the myriad activities of the past two days. There had been secret conferences with Adalph and Kilar in the Outside. There had been the hurried assembling of free gladiators. Plans had to be made clear-cut and final.

Jonnath thought it more work than fighting for his life in the arena, and said so at one point.

Kilar Gri provided the rebuke. "We are making here today only the first step in what could begin to be the end of Zarmithan expansionism. If we win this struggle here, it will be but the first of many. All of us here have agreed we will accept the Emperor Shaikon's offer to utilize us as a special Free Army operating in coordination with his own struggles against Zarmith. The work we have before us is infinitely greater than anything we have done in the arena—or will do today. We have a lifetime apiece to spend in making the Star Guards wish they had not tried to make us their slaves!"

It wasn't really that satisfying a reply, though Jonnath, and then he caught sight of the spearing flame from the sky.

The shattered dome smashed down with a roar. Jonnath watched on a portable solido as the arena cameras suddenly swung about aimlessly for a moment, then focussed on a small scout craft at rest on the arena sands. In the background the audience of a quarter of a million began to stir like an army of ants trapped on flypaper. The noise rose.

And in the crowd there spangled into being a thousand, ten thousand, fifty thousand forcefields, as the Star Guards present were signaled to Alert.

Then the plates around the nose of the tail-perching craft slid aside. A squat ungainly machine with a lone man at its controls was revealed.

The machine began to hum; a pale blue glow slowly formed around it, then expanded. First it touched the force barriers between the audience and the pit—and the barriers radiated upward into the ultraviolet, and winked out. Clouds of smoke arose almost immediately from the emergency generators concealed just inside the pit walls, as they attempted to take over the screens and were themselves wrenched by the new weapon into explosion and ruin.

The pale blue glow expanded farther—and as it touched the Star Guards' crimson-glowing fields they winked out by the tens of thousands. Clouds of smoke arose from their portable generators, and shouts and screams tore the air. Many of the generators then exploded, wreaking new havoc among the crowds.

Up from the arena pits streamed ten thousand gladiators; they stormed over the walls of the arena on ladders, and began cutting their way through those guards still able to fight, and those who somehow had failed to activate their screens before Shaikon's invention had attacked.

Other gladiators took up strategic positions outside the amphitheater, to fight off outside attack and to prevent guards from fighting their way outside.

At this point transmission from the arena ceased. Jonnath cursed again.

Thereafter to the end all was confusion. Despite precautions, a group of several thousand Star Guards had gathered, and had forced their way out, to be met by another three or four thousand representing the rest of the Tansavar base personnel, who had not attended the games that day for various reasons. The influence of the blue field extended throughout the city, and the Star Guard fields were still useless. It was time to act.

Jonnath's attack with his two hundred would have been suicidal within moments had they been fighting in an open space. But this was inside the city, and though Tansavar's streets and avenues were wide, they were not so wide as to allow the confused masses of Star Guards room to fight these assailants to their rear.

What the Emperor Shaikon in Ziaphar, wrapped in his furs and cloth-of-gold in his palace of translucent green stone and seated on his throne of solid gold, had suspected was true. Without their invincible energy fields of patterned electricity the Star Guards were by and large mediocre fighters. They had grown soft in the fifteen years since the development of the personal field, trusting to their armament and letting their skills rust.

Jonnath's two hundred carved their way through three times their number, causing great havoc among the remaining five thousand. These variously strove to attack their attackers or to proceed toward the arena and rescue those who remained there; the result was chaos, and through that chaos strode Jonnath and his men, unswervable avengers.

Eventually, though, the five thousand Star Guards formed a more coherent fighting unit as they reached the great plaza in front of the arena.

Now the tide could turn, Jonnath realized. His own force could no longer hope to defeat the guards, whose military discipline was beginning to assert itself. And the gladiators from the arena, having wiped out most of the guards inside, were streaming out into the square and attacking the guards in small groups. They were naturally being cut to pieces.

Would M'rongovorth never arrive?

Then down the city-splitting Avenue of Princes, in an irresistible battering charge, came a stampede of bisfas beasts, a solid mass of thousand kilo monsters heading straight for the side of the Star Guards' position in the Grand Plaza.

Willan Vis sat on top of M'rongovorth, who was really leading the charge. Willan was firing two Nangee flashers simultaneously and howling incoherently into an ampli-phone.

It was too much for the Star Guards. Some fought, some quit, but the main battle was over in another fifteen minutes.

The city of Tansavar was in agony. Spotty solido trans-mission had been resumed by a band of the rebels; it showed the disastrous effects of Shaikon's plot, which had worked perfectly.

Mobs of slaves roamed the avenues and streets, plundering and setting fires. Many of the gladiators who were not Kalvaran broke away and began drinking and looting. The citizens were in panic after the slaughter in the arena, for while the gladiators had tried to kill only Star Guards, many others had been killed also. Jonnath stared gloomily at his small solido while, underneath him, M'rongovorth forced a way through the wrecked streets. A detachment of Kalvaran gladiators followed him, keep-ing close.

Time! Will I have time! Jonnath thought desperately, knowing that Shaikon's freighter to pick them up had al-ready landed; Star Guard reinforcements could arrive from Zarmith itself in less than three more Standard hours. The rest of the Kalvaran gladiators were stolidly at work destroying Star Guard installations and generally wreaking morale shattering havoc.

The Lady Tza's palace in Tansavar was isolated from the affairs of the city by wide grassy grounds and a large stone wall. Jonnath and his fifty Kalvaran studied it from a small office building across the way from the back of the palace.

"We don't have time to plan fancy maneuvers," said Jonnath, after a moment. Quickly he gave a series of orders.

A dozen gladiators set their Nangees on blast intensity, then at a signal fired simultaneously at the wall just be-side a steel gateway which was locked.

There was a shattering boom and a great cloud of dust rolled swiftly toward the palace from the wall, propelled by the aftereffects of the Nangees. The wall was in ruins over a front of five meters.

Several Star Guards in faded red cloth uniforms ap-

168

peared in the breech and attempted to fire, but were beamed down immediately. A detachment of five gladiators darted across the street, took up covering positions in the rubble, then signaled back an all clear.

"They're setting up last ditch defenses in the palace itself," said Jonnath aloud to no one in particular. M'rongovorth growled and moved forward across the street.

Inside the palace the fighting was bitter and bloody, as confused in miniature as the general confusion outside; but presently Jonnath realized that his gladiators were carrying the day. Taking a half-dozen with him for contingencies, he struck out in search of anyone who could tell him where Krith Vaggar was. Some of the corridors were narrow; the bisfas had to stay behind, and M'rongovorth growled again, in protest, but did not dare to speak aloud among the intermingling of strangers.

After ten minutes of searching, Jonnath found himself in a darkened wing of the palace. "Every room is suspect," he said then. "Blast every lock, kick it open, and stand back."

It took five doors. The fifth swung open before Jonnath could fire. "Come in, dom you," said a man's deep voice from inside. "I know when I'm beaten." The voice was familiar.

A man dressed in crimson was sitting on a couch drinking from a mug of what smelled like Lashkari ale. He wore the black gloves of a captain in the Star Guards.

The face, that was familiar too. It was Krith Vaggar.

"Dom the Lady, then," said Krith, and took a drink from the mug. "Ordered me to stand and fight. Wouldn't let me take the secret exit. Man there with a flasher to stop me. Crux her, I say."

He looked sideways at Jonnath, then pressed a button on his belt. "Captain Vaggar. All guards in the palace, cease firing. Lieutenant Youm, acknowledge." The sound of distant firing echoed in the small room, then died away. A tinny voice said, "Cease fire accomplished, sir. Further orders?"

"Dom it, surrender, you fool!"

Vaggar jabbed another button on his belt, glowered at his mug, and drank again. Then he peered up at Jonnath, who stood there with drawn flasher, several gladiators behind him in the doorway. "I'm unarmed, unless you want me to surrender my sword too," said Vaggar, a touch of sarcasm in his voice. He stood. "Shall we go?"

"Not just yet, Vaggar," said Jonnath, his voice low and steady. "There are some things I want of you first . . ."

There was unsteadiness in the captain's voice as he answered, his words hurrying over each other. "Perhaps we can deal with each other, then. I have plans, lad, plans—for your men too, as well as you, if you'll join me in getting out of this dom palace as soon as possible."

Jonnath said nothing, sizing up his man.

"One of the frontier planets; I've got it all lined up—a base of operations to start my own kingdom! I've got almost as much money as I need. With fighters like you beside me, we could be invincible! We could carve out an empire! I watched the uprising—fantastic fighters you are. And what chance have you here? Zarmith will have a thousand ships here before stardown. You'll be wiped out to the last man."

Vaggar smeared his sweating face with his faded sleeve, and Jonnath spoke at last.

"First, you have a girl that I want."

Vaggar looked genuinely surprised. "I offer you an empire and you want . . . a *girl?*"

"Not any girl. This is one you took from the city of Kallor, during the rape of Kalvar—"

Now Vaggar was astonished. "I have such a girl with me—take her, with my . . . blessings!" His face quirked in an involuntary wry smile, and he clapped his hands loudly. "Though why you want this one . . . nothing but a cheap Kalvaran slut . . ."

Jonnath stepped forward to strike the man, but footsteps sounded then from an inner corridor—a girl's light footsteps. Jonnath turned to Sheira as she entered the room.

It was not Sheira.

It was Triez.

Too shocked to speak himself, Jonnath listened as the story was pieced out. Triez had been badly wounded when Borlat Vorz had shot her down. After Sheira and Jonnath had been taken away, Captain Vaggar had inspected Kilar Gri's mansion to make sure there were no others

170

hidden there, and then discovered that the girl was not dead.

She was only eleven, but Krith Vaggar's tastes covered a broad spectrum, and he took her along. After recovering from her wound, she became the captain's mistress. At fourteen, she looked twenty, Jonnath thought, and he noticed the way she clung to the captain's arm.

"When this is over," he said then, "I'll take you to the Ten Star Complex. There will be some money for you, though not much, and—"

"Money!" Triez laughed. "I have what I need." And she clung tighter to the captain; then, seeing the perplexed look on Jonnath's face, she kissed Vaggar.

The captain disengaged her from him roughly, his face clouding up. "Get out," he said. "Go to the Ten Stars or back to the sty you came from. We talk of serious things now."

Sheira forgotten momentarily, Jonnath tried desperately to reach Triez. "What kind of life is this? You see, he despises you. He casts you aside. Come and—"

"He is but one man," said Triez calmly. Was there a touch of arrogance? "There are many others like him— and one he has been jealous of . . ." She stepped away from Krith Vaggar. ". . . with very good reason!"

Vaggar growled and swiped at her. "Dom, the world's gone mad. We balance life and death and empires, and you—"

Triez' youth glimmered forth for a moment, and she simply stuck out her tongue at the captain, who was swaying now from anger and the effects of the ale.

Roaring incoherently with rage, Krith Vaggar moved toward the girl and raised his arm. Jonnath handed his rifle to a gladiator behind him, then stepped between the two.

"Dom!" said the captain, enraged past reason, and he drew his short dress sword. "Let it be swords, then, and guard your throat, krol!"

Krith Vaggar was a good swordsman. Jonnath smoothly moved away from his first wild swing and drew his own sword—only to have Vaggar knock it spinning out of his hands as it cleared his scabbard.

One of the gladiators raised his Nangee flasher, and Vaggar froze.

"No!" shouted Jonnath as he darted for his sword in the corner. "I'll deal with him *my* way!"

A great dark joy filled his heart as his hand closed around the hilt of his sword. Now to earn payment for his father and his mother, for what Vaggar had forced Triez to become, for those years in the arena—*now!"*

He raised his sword and awaited Vaggar. Their blades met, and clashed discordantly in the small room.

Krith Vaggar was a head shorter than Jonnath, and not in peak condition. The smell of ale on his breath was strong, and he had trouble with his footing.

But he was strong as a bisfas, Jonnath realized, and rage had added more strength to his arm. For long seconds the battle was almost in Vaggar's favor.

Then the captain faltered and missed an easy riposte. In the next exchange he missed another. Relentlessly, Jonnath began to force him across the room, and backed him up against the wall.

"Now," he shouted, knocking the captain's sword out of his hands almost disdainfully, "now you pay for—"

The catalog of injuries was on his tongue, when there was a screamed "No!" from Triez. Dashing across the room she grabbed Jonnath by the elbow—but forced his sword full into Krith Vaggar's throat!

She screamed again, as a look of puzzlement more than pain crossed the captain's face. His hands reached falteringly upward to his throat . . . and froze in that position as his knees buckled, and he toppled forward headfirst onto the stone floor.

Jonnath stood for a moment, dazed, then, panic-stricken, he kneeled to the floor and turned the body over hastily. Empty eyes stared up at him as he babbled, "Don't die yet, dom you, you've got to know *why* you suffer—my parents and . . ."

His voice died away. There was no doubt about it—Krith Vaggar was already dead; he couldn't hear a word Jonnath was saying. *Vengeance,* thought Jonnath bitterly, and the word echoed in his mind; *is this vengeance?*

Jonnath stood as Triez crumpled onto Vaggar's body, weeping hysterically. Vague desperate thoughts scrambled around his brain in meaningless patterns; all that was clear was that he'd killed the man who murdered his mother and father, and hadn't even been able to tell him who he was avenging . . . and Triez, it seemed, had loved him, in spite of her words.

He put his hands on her shoulders. "He isn't worth your tears," he said. "He's the last man who could have told me about Sheira, and . . . he was the man who killed your father."

"I used to dream nightmares of him," Triez said in a dull voice as she hunched up on her knees and stared down at the body. "In my dreams it was always he who killed my father and your parents, always he tracking me across nightmare deserts and jungles . . . and yet when I woke I could not believe it. I . . . loved him.

"But I will love his successor just as much. Sheira never had understood—"

Jonnath felt sweat in the palms of his hands. "Sheira . . ."

Triez looked up. "She always thought herself the lucky one, living the comfortable upstairs life. She doesn't know how it can be, living with and loving a man like this, following him as he climbs—"

"Sheira—upstairs *where?*" he asked urgently.

Triez looked at him blankly. "Why, here, of course! She's a personal handmaiden to the Lady Tza. And what she's going to do now that the mistress has fled . . ." A small smile crossed Triez' face. "Well, *I* know what *I'm* going to do . . ."

"Dom you—" he started to say, but could not continue. A feeling like sunrise was welling up within him. "Upstairs, you say? Sheira?"

He laughed aloud then, turned, and brushed the two gladiators in the doorway aside, and went running, running, running, down the corridors and up the flights of stairs, and found her at last, and they threw their arms around each other and laughed with the joy of it all being over . . .

THE END

A new solution to the
puzzling problem of the UFO!

FLYING SAUCERS:
HOAX OR REALITY?

By L. Jerome Stanton

The author of this book is not a believer.
He is not a non-believer.
He is a scientifically trained writer with vast experience in this and related fields. He is unbiased, but exceedingly curious. He has sifted through the reports of the Air Force and the independent UFO research groups. By applying his own scientific knowledge, he has unearthed some **startling** facts never before disclosed!

This is by far the most informative book on the subject today.

Absorbing as a good mystery novel—but make no mistake —this is fact.

B50-761   50¢

FREE BOOKS!

*Choose any 4 exciting Belmont Books listed
below and receive the fifth book absolutely free!
Choose 7 books and get 2 additional books free!*